CU01266937

DIRTY SLIDE

LAUREN BLAKELY
KD CASEY

NOTHING TO LOSE PRODUCTIONS

ALSO BY LAUREN BLAKELY

Sex and Other Shiny Objects

One Night Stand-In

Lucky In Love Series

Best Laid Plans

The Feel Good Factor

Nobody Does It Better

Unzipped

Always Satisfied Series

Satisfaction Guaranteed

Instant Gratification

Overnight Service

Never Have I Ever

PS It's Always Been You

Special Delivery

The Sexy Suit Series

Lucky Suit

Birthday Suit

From Paris With Love

Wanderlust

Part-Time Lover

One Love Series

The Sexy One

The Only One

The Hot One

The Knocked Up Plan

Come As You Are

Sports Romance

Most Valuable Playboy

Most Likely to Score

Standalones

Stud Finder

The V Card

The Real Deal

Unbreak My Heart

The Break-Up Album

The Caught Up in Love Series

*The Pretending Plot (*previously called *Pretending He's Mine*)

The Dating Proposal

*The Second Chance Plan (*previously called *Caught Up In Us)*

The Private Rehearsal (previously called *Playing With Her Heart*)

Seductive Nights Series

Night After Night

After This Night

One More Night

A Wildly Seductive Night

ALSO BY KD CASEY

One True Outcome

Unwritten Rules

ABOUT

Don't play dirty.

That's the code I live by on and off the field.

The other?

Don't get distracted.

Not by the media, not by hookups, and definitely not by our rival team's ridiculously charming star player, who loves to whisper dirty nothings to me every time we play ball.

And sure, his offers are tempting, but he's the love 'em and leave 'em type, and I want the real thing.

So I resist.

But the night he steals second on me in the biggest game of the year, the guy's a whole lot harder to ignore. Especially after a filthy postgame kiss leaves me wanting all the things I can't have.

What's the risk in playing dirty just one time?

NOTE FROM AUTHORS

A Note from Lauren to Readers,

When I finished reading KD Casey's debut novel *Unwritten Rules* I was so impressed that I asked her to co-write a fun little scene with me between two baseball players. We'd both written baseball romances so this made perfect sense. We had such a great time with these characters that a short scene turned into a sexy, flirty, dirty stand-alone novella that we love. I hope you enjoy reading Dirty Slide as much as we enjoyed writing it!

Xoxo

Lauren

. . .

A Note from KD Casey to Readers,

I was ecstatic when Lauren reached out to me about potentially collaborating on a story. I loved the *Men of Summer* series, and jumped at the opportunity to create a new baseball romance. What started as a short story soon grew with the characters (which is one of the joys of writing!). We truly had a blast writing this and hope you have the same reading!

Play ball!

KD

DIRTY SLIDE

Want to be the first to learn of sales, new releases, preorders and special freebies from Lauren Blakely and KD Casey? Sign up for our MM VIP mailing list here!

CHRIS GARNETT

September

I really should stop flirting with Josh Spencer.

Truly, I should.

But, c'mon, he flirts right back just as hard.

Like at the golf tournament earlier this year. The dude stole glances at me seven times on the course. Three more at the luncheon after.

Yes, I counted.

And that was a whole lot of eye-fucking.

Which is fine by me. I don't mind being ogled by sexy, driven men I'd like to take out on a date. Bonus that we play the same sport and *get* the demands of the job.

But I haven't asked him to grab a drink yet. Asking a guy out is like waiting for your pitch. You've got to have patience and find just the right moment.

Maybe I'll have the chance tonight when I step into the batter's box in the fifth inning of a September game against our rivals.

The Union pitcher throws a fastball that paints the corner of the strike zone. A good pitch, except I put an even better swing on it and send it deep into the outfield.

And pull up on second base.

It's a warm night. A sheen of sweat streaks his temples. His jersey sits close against his chest. *Hello, hottie.*

I catch my breath from hustling out a double, stripping my batting gloves off and stuffing them in my back pocket. "Busy night out here for ya, Spencer?"

"Hi, Garnett," he sighs, comically loud.

"Nice to see you too."

"We really need to stop meeting like this." He pretends to be all business, but I can see the twinkle in his deep brown eyes.

"I'd agree, but I do like hitting doubles against your team," I say since it's my second of the night.

"Wish I could say the same," Josh says.

"Hit a triple when you're up next, and you can come visit me."

"Count on that." Josh's lips curve into a grin, one he quickly schools.

"Aww, you're looking forward to seeing me," I tease.

That earns me a well-deserved eye roll. "Obviously." Josh stares off at the mound for a beat, then gives me a quick glance as he says drily, "It'd mean I'm on third base."

Ah, hell. I can't resist. "Is third base your favorite?" I ask, laying it on thick in the innuendo department since that's what I do.

In slo-mo, he turns his gaze to me once more, giving me the full effect of those gorgeous brown eyes. "No. I prefer all the way," he says.

Well, then.

Our next hitter is up. I take a few steps off second base, readying myself, refocusing on the game in front of me and not the man.

And when my teammate sends me home on a line drive single, I figure I'll just hunt for another chance with my cross-town rival.

It comes the next night when Josh hustles into third base, where I'm fielding.

He takes his time looking down at the bag, then up at me. "Yeah, I guess I do like third base after all," he says, and yup, this feels like my pitch.

But seconds later, the guy's flying toward home plate. And when the ninth inning ends, his team wins.

Despite being our rivals, I'm friendly with a couple of guys on the Union and plan to head out with them tonight. But the one I'm most interested in seeing right now is the guy who makes my pulse pound. The good luck gods shine on me as I wait at their clubhouse entrance.

The sexy second baseman for my rival team exits first, looking damn good in jeans and a charcoal gray Henley. And all that late-night stubble.

"Good game," I say.

"Yeah, I like it when we beat you," he says.

"I bet you do." For a few seconds, I eye him up and down. "You taking off right now?"

"Yeah, what about you?"

"There's a bunch of us going out to play pool. If you want to join and grab a beer after," I say since that's casual enough. Josh lifts a brow, like he's curious, considering my offer, but I don't want to come on too strong, so I add, "You know, just for fun."

And something about that last word shuts him down. *Fun.*

His face goes stoic—kind of frowny. "I have a thing in the morning. So, yeah. I should probably go."

And Josh takes off.

I guess that settles that.

Except, it doesn't when I see him again in the last game of the year.

2

JOSH SPENCER

October

Baseball has a ton of rules, but some are so obvious they don't even need to be written down.

Like, say, when you're manning second base, maybe don't get distracted by the sexy AF guy on first. Especially when he plays for the opposing team. Double that when it's the top of the sixth inning of the last game of the World freaking Series.

Too bad my brain didn't get the message since I would really like to follow that rule right the hell now. This is only the biggest game of my career, and there will be zero flirting tonight. That's a brand-new addendum to my unwritten rule.

As our relief pitcher trots in from the bullpen, I do an inventory of the moment to get my mind off my inconvenient attraction to Chris Garnett.

It's October. The air is cool, the stadium packed. I've been playing almost every day since early March. An endless season, except it'll end in a few innings with one team wearing the ring and the other wearing the loss.

Ideally, Chris's team will lose, mine will win, and I'll end up with a ring.

So I cut myself some slack, then double down on my focus. As our pitcher throws to the guy at the plate, I do my job keeping an eye on Chris, dancing off first base, ready to steal if my focus wanes.

Like I'll let him swipe second without a fight.

My concentration doesn't even flicker for a second. But it takes less than that for our pitcher to fire off a curveball. For Chris to take off running down the base path toward me and for our catcher to scoop the ball from the dirt and hurl it my way. With a feet-first slide that sprays dirt on my pinstriped uniform pants, Chris's spiked cleats tear into my ankle.

What the fuck?

It hurts, like being stabbed with a fork. I jump back reflexively, enough that I can't lay down a tag in time, and the ump calls him safe. Words form in my head, like *are you fucking serious,* but they die on my tongue because I might get thrown out if I argue with the umpire.

Argue with Chris though? Gladly.

"That's a dirty fucking play, Garnett," I spit out, staring down at the guy who's trying to ruin my night. The guy who already invades my after-midnight . . . fantasies.

"You sure about that, Spencer?" Chris's voice is all casual innocence, but his cool blue eyes roam up and down me as he stands.

"It was, and you know it," I add, but then remind myself of my own golden rule—*no distractions.* I won't be distracted by this man and his heated gaze. This man who's now inches away and smells like sweat and determination, and fantasies I won't let myself have.

Chris just shrugs as he wipes dirt off his pants, gives a cocky smile. "Let me tell you what I know—pretty sure you slid the same way earlier in the series."

I won't let him get to me, even though my pulse surges with him this close. I say nothing. Just grind my teeth.

But Chris is chatty. Personable. A media darling. So he keeps talking. "And they didn't call it that way. Maybe you're mistaking it for something else."

I shake my head in frustration. He could have broken my ankle sliding in like that. He was *this* close. He knows it too because he's flashing that winning smile. The one he flings my way in other games when he flirts and teases. The one that's, evidently, been tricking every umpire all season.

Of course, he's a nice guy. His name is fucking Chris. They're always the nice guys. A good *clean* player, despite that dirty slide.

Yeah, right.

I was fooled too.

He turns the spotlight of his magnetic grin fully toward me. "So quiet tonight. Everything going okay . . . Spencer?" Chris goads like we're not playing in the World Series in front of fifty thousand spectators. Like he didn't just spike my ankle. And like he didn't just say my last name like he's rolling it around on his tongue, as if we're on a date, not on the diamond.

Like we're just having *fun.*

But fun isn't what I'm after. "It will be when you walk into the losing clubhouse tonight," I mutter.

"Don't count on that." Chris laughs—a rumbly, sexy kind. "But don't worry. I'll be gentle on y'all when I slide home. Unless . . ."

He smirks at the unstated question, but it rings in my head anyway. I look away as our pitcher readies himself for the next pitch.

"But I bet you don't want me to be gentle," Chris adds.

Dude can read my mind, and I'm about to tell him to fuck off when there's an ear-splitting whack, the ball smoked off the Gothams hitter's bat and deep into the outfield. Chris barrels toward third, but not without a final streaked "told you so" in his wake.

That guy.

When he crosses home plate several seconds later, he punches the air, then spins around, and . . . points.

My. Way.

And I swear the asshole winks too.

Then struts into the dugout.

And I'm livid.

To think I was *this close* to saying yes to his offer last month.

But by the seventh inning, I'm upset. By the eighth, I'm nauseous. By the ninth, I'm wiping my hands across my blurred vision and telling myself I'm wiping away sweat. And then, the inevitable happens.

We lose. There's no way around it. And Chris, fucking good guy Chris, scores what turns out to be the winning run.

Figures.

After, we retreat to our dugout as the Gothams celebrate on the field. They're stripping off their jerseys, pulling on T-shirts that declare themselves the champions of the entire baseball world, chomping cigars, embracing.

Our clubhouse feels like walking into a mausoleum. Plastic sheeting hangs above each player's stall. Protection against champagne we'll never get to spray. Some guys are on the phone with their families, voices low, sad. Our short-stop, a rookie who's barely old enough to drink, cries.

But I'm not sad anymore. Whatever tears I had have dried themselves. Now I'm furious because they beat us dirty. Thanks to a guy I can't stop thinking about.

This is the kind of anger that survives a shower, the kind that carries into the post-game press conference. Reporters stick microphones and recording devices in my face. All their questions collapse into one: How does it *feel* to lose a World Series?

Pretty fucking shitty.

"How about that slide Garnett laid down in the sixth?" a reporter asks.

He's the last guy I want to talk about, so I try to call up the script for how this is supposed to go, so I can be a gracious loser. Except my ankle hurts. My ego hurts. Whatever nice thing I'm supposed to summon about *nice* Chris, who plays the game *right*, stalls between my lungs and my throat.

"Well, the call went his way, so it must have been the right one," I say, playing mostly by the PR rulebook. Except, an image of Chris flashes before me, him wanting to grab a beer just for fun. Then one of him taunting *I told you so* that makes it clear who he is. Screw the script. "But I don't think there's a place for that kind of play in the game anymore, especially from a guy like Garnett."

The reporters all draw inward, brought closer by the rarity of an honest answer. One bobs a mic near my face as a request to elaborate.

Adjectives for Chris pop into my head: Arrogant. Hot-headed. Just plain *hot*. Then, I move beyond adjectives as I picture that golden-brown hair. Those cool eyes. That square jawline. None of which I say. I'm not in the closet. That's not the issue. I'm just not going to broadcast to the whole country that I fantasize about the guy who just cost me my dream. "He's supposed to be a role model, right?"

The question hangs there. My implication is clear. Maybe that'll put at least a little tarnish on their trophy.

I'm stopped or saved by our media relations person who shoots an arched eyebrow and a *scram* look at the reporters. "Let's let these guys get cleaned up," Maritza says, despite the fact that my hair is still dripping from the shower.

The reporters leave eventually. It's silent in their wake. Noise from a celebration in the visiting team's clubhouse drifts into ours. It's a celebration that will last all through the night and probably through the off-season.

Chris is probably leading the party. He's probably covered in champagne. All over his chest. Great, now I'm annoyed and turned on —a lethal combo.

My jaw is set hard, and I don't say a word, so the guys give me a wide berth. Except for Zach Glasser, our catcher, who settles in the chair next to mine.

He's kind of a quiet guy normally. Even

now, it takes him a while to say whatever it is he's gearing up to.

"Slide looked clean," he says finally.

"He swiped that bag off you too. Aren't you pissed off?"

"Sometimes, you lose. That's just how it is." He looks down at where my hand is resting, my knuckles white with tension. "Don't do anything rash, Spence."

I think of Chris and his unrestrained smile and the punch of his cleats in my ankle. The way he plays like he's got nothing to lose. I guess he doesn't anymore. He's won it all. "I'm not the one with poor impulse control," I say, though it feels like I might be. Like whatever in me that says *focus, focus, focus* crumbled when Chris stole his way onto my base.

Though, maybe it's been crumbling all season since the golf tournament. And every time I ran into him on or off the field since then. With every look. Every word.

All that ends tonight.

"Remember that time in August the Cougars' pinch hitter slid into your feet first? You weren't half as mad, and the guy could barely run."

Ouch.

"It wasn't the World Series," I say in my defense. But it sounds weak even to my ears.

"Sure," Glasser says. "That must be all it is." He thumps me twice on the shoulder then gets up. "Take it easy."

I wish easygoing were my style.

But I'm not like Chris.

Eventually, I drag myself out of the clubhouse and toward the players' parking lot. Except when I get there, someone's leaning against the door of my car: The last person I want to see right now, flush with victory and cocky as hell and smiling like he's on top of the world. A smile I want to wipe off his face. Or kiss off. And I don't know which is worse.

3

CHRIS

I've only fantasized about winning a World Series since I was five.

When I was younger, I imagined hitting the game-winning homer, the crowd cheering, my team lifting me on their shoulders.

As I got older, my dreams grew up.

Playing hard. Winning here in New York and then enjoying the hell out of the victory. We're talking parties, champagne, debauchery, the world ours for the taking, no pleasure too great to be denied.

Except the guy I've had my sights on all season long just called me a dirty fucking player on national TV.

I grab a bottle of champagne from a laundry cart full of them—because I earned the hell out of this expensive bottle, and I have plans for it—then stalk through the tunnels to the players' lot. Along the way, I replay on my phone that damn interview he just gave.

I can't believe my rival insinuated the same shit on air that he breathed to me on base. It's one thing to talk trash on the field. It's another to do it in public.

It makes me want to throw down with him. Or throw him across my bed.

Both, and that's messing with me.

This isn't the first time I've thought about the second baseman for the Union. Ever since that golf tournament, I was drawn to him, to his dry humor, to his intensity, and to the way he snuck glances at me. The way he has in every game this season. He stares at me like he wants to eat me for dinner.

Feeling is mutual, Josh.

And I'm sure he's been playing a reel in his head too of what a night together might look like. Ballplayers are visual people. We have to imagine each at bat, each pitch, each play. So I get the full jumbotron visualization of Josh Spencer's big body up against the wall in my apartment. Then down on his knees in my living room, so I can tug hard on that thick, dark hair. Then on my bed, spread out, miles of tanned skin for my mouth to explore.

Any or all of the above, the kind of celebration that extends into the next day. Or, some traitorous part of me whispers, *even longer than that*.

But first, I have a major bone to pick with him. Maybe he needs a lesson in choosing his words carefully. For instance, gasping my name would be a much better use of his lush lips.

Outside in the players' lot, I find his black Tesla easily and lean against it. Waiting. Running my thumb over the top of the champagne, I stare at the moon, then at the emptying lot as other New York Union guys leave.

Some wave to me. Some flip me the bird.

I blow them all kisses. Since tonight I won the trophy, and everything is awesome.

Except for this sitch with Spencer.

Speak of the enemy. The guy who called me dirty strides across the lot, stopping in his tracks when he's five feet away.

"Let me guess. You came to gloat," Josh says, a hard edge to his voice.

Funny, I thought I wanted to set the record straight, but it's really hard to toe that line when all your childhood dreams just came true. "A little," I admit with a grin since he's not wrong.

"Save it, Garnett," Josh mutters.

And I take that as an invitation. "I've been saving it all season."

A line digs into his forehead. "What are you talking about?" Then he seems to think better of it, walking closer, lifting the key fob. "Forget it. Don't care."

Bullshit.

I don't move, even though he's in my space now. And why not get to the bottom of things? That's part of my plan to celebrate. To deal with the shit he said, then take him to bed. Once and for all.

Those are my plans. Plain and simple. We both want it.

Josh's gaze drifts down to the bottle I'm holding. I set it on the ground like we're just gonna have a little heart-to-heart in a dim parking lot when I smell like victory champagne and cigar smoke. A reminder of everything I just won. Everything he lost.

And maybe everything we can still have later tonight.

I set a hand on his hard chest. His breath hitches, then he goes still. "So it seems you think I played dirty?"

"You did," he says, but it's a little wobbly. Like maybe he's not quite certain.

"I don't think you know what it means to

play dirty, Spencer," I say in a low voice, fingers gripping his shirt.

He doesn't pull away. He just lets out a harsh breath, close to a pant. "You're a world champion. Why does it matter what I think?"

"The better question is, why do you want to think the worst of me all of a sudden?"

Josh scoffs, then licks his lips. "Trust me. I'm not thinking of you at all."

"You were definitely talking about me on TV tonight."

His face shutters, transforming back to the locked-up Josh Spencer who called me dirty to the press. "I thought you weren't that kind of player."

"The kind who's a world champion?"

He seethes, huffing through his nostrils, then lets loose. "The kind who thinks it doesn't matter how you play so long as you win. But I guess you want it both ways—to bend the rules and to not get called out for it."

But I don't feel like debating the game anymore. "Seems like you've thought about the kind of player I am a lot. Or, really, just about . . . *me*."

Up close, his eyes are a ludicrous brown. They widen slightly in surprise. *Gotcha.*

But he's not a competitor for nothing. He

recovers quickly. "I think about a lot of things, Garnett. Right now, I'm thinking about whether there's traffic on the Harlem River Drive, so don't flatter yourself."

"Take I-87. It's faster," I whisper. "If you're in a rush to get home, that is."

"Thanks," he says, breath a little shaky. "Appreciate the tip."

But maybe he's not in such a hurry after all. The man isn't moving, so I make the next move, admitting something since maybe that'll get us closer to bed. "Funny thing is, you play just as hard. You leave it all on the field too," I say.

Josh takes a beat, maybe to process that admission, his lips twitching in a hint of a grin. "You watch me?" he asks, and with those three words, his tone downshifts. For the first time, there's a flirty vibe to it, one that might tell me to fuck off. Or order me to my knees. And we're getting warmer.

"Yeah, I do," I say, my fist clutching the fabric now. "I definitely have my eyes on you and you know it."

Josh looks down, then back up, his eyes locking with mine. "I've noticed," he murmurs.

"You've been looking back." It isn't a question.

He gives the barest of nods.

And for a few hot seconds, the temperature in me spikes.

The air crackles.

I know what we both need. "I've got an idea, Spencer."

"What's that?" His voice pitches up with dirty hope.

I jerk him closer. There's an inch between us. One more move, and we'll be smashed together, hip to hip, grinding it out.

That's what he wants. That's what I want. "You and me. This champagne. My place," I say, putting it out there for the first time, so there's zero confusion. This is an invitation for one person only, not for a casual thing. Because the one thing Josh and I aren't is casual about each other.

Josh swallows roughly, breathing hard. My gaze drifts down to his neatly trimmed beard, to the way his throat pulses. Yeah, his body's an open book too, and the pages are telling me he's so damn aroused right now.

Join the club, Josh.

"Let me get this straight," he rasps out, clearly trying to fight off the gravel in his voice. "You think that after all the shit you pulled tonight, I'd let you suck my dick?"

"I don't just think you'd let me. I think

you want me to. Badly. And like I said, I can be gentle."

"Maybe I don't want it gentle," he counters, with a hiss.

Yes. Fucking yes.

"Now we're getting somewhere," I say.

Josh shakes his head. "You might want to keep the cork in that champagne, Garnett."

But I'm a hopeful guy, and I'm so damn close to solving the problem of him and me. Because he's *not* pushing me away. He's *not* tearing my hand off his shirt.

He *is* staring at my lips.

So I close the distance with one more jerk of his fabric.

He's right up against me, his hard-on pressed against mine.

His breath hitches, and he dips his face.

Then groans. Low and filthy.

That. Sound.

Right there.

I lean into him, my lips barely brushing his as I whisper, "Like I said, I'll show you what it means to play dirty."

Josh doesn't say anything for a second, but I'm willing to bet comebacks are forming in that head. Comebacks at odds with his cock pressed against me. "No doubt you would," he says, barely audible. "But I'm going home."

Which would be more convincing if he actually got in his car. The key fob chirps the doors open once more.

And yet, he's still right up against me.

"You're going home, Spencer. So are you inviting me over then?" I brush my lips across his jaw, dragging them over the prickle of his beard. "We can beat the traffic. Take the I-87," I suggest.

Savoring the gasp that comes from him.

The press of his hips into mine.

The feel of his arousal against me.

Most of all, the way he lifts his chin just so, just a millimeter, giving me access.

And I take what he's offering, as my lips travel down his neck, to his collarbone, then I lick. And press a hot, open-mouthed kiss on his skin.

He moans.

Yes.

I want all his noises, all his sighs, murmurs and grunts. So I rope my free hand around his hip, cover his firm ass, and tug him against me.

The sounds he makes are criminal as I grind against him, and he answers me right back with his body moving with mine.

My god, the things I want to do to Josh, for Josh. With Josh.

I could probably convince him, with my tongue, and hands and cock. But I want to hear it from the man himself. That he wants this, wants me, as much as I want him.

I break apart, meet his gaze. "So, what's it gonna be tonight?"

His brown eyes are hazy, and they have that intoxicated look that tells me he wants all the same things. Me having him. Him having me.

But then he blinks, breathes out hard, and steps back. His nails press into his palm. "Not in the mood tonight." Said like he's arguing with himself. "Some other time."

He cuts past me, gets into his car, and drives away.

Leaving me with my erection, this bottle of champagne, and a whole lot of dirty dreams unfulfilled.

4

JOSH

February

Commentators like to say that baseball is a game of short memories. You win some and flush the rest. That's bullshit. There's no forgetting losing the World Series. On TV. As part of the first "Subway Series"—two New York teams playing each other—in more than twenty years.

Also, people in this city aren't exactly prone to letting things go. As it turns out, I'm not either. I haven't forgotten a single detail from that night in late October.

Especially the ones that happened *after* the last out.

The day I'm supposed to leave for spring

training, I peel myself out of bed. My apartment is big for Manhattan and small for anywhere else. Now, it's dark from the blackout curtains I use during the season to sleep late, rendering it either cozy or claustrophobic.

I wish I'd slept late. Wish I'd forgotten the blinking calendar appointment on my schedule.

Trouble is, I haven't stopped thinking about this day. In an hour, I have a photoshoot. With Chris.

Groan.

How the hell do I act with him? Like I didn't totally want him to take me apart last time I saw him? Like I didn't want to punch him? Like I'm just totally cool being this attracted to the guy who stole my World Series ring?

My agent says that it'll be good for me to lean into the rivalry. My teammates say it'll be therapeutic to see Chris in controlled circumstances.

My buddy Grant has simpler advice every time I see him.

After I make myself more or less presentable, I meet the catcher for the San Francisco Cougars for a cup of joe. After a quick once over, he shakes his head, then serves up what he's been telling me for the last few months when it comes to Chris Garnett.

"Dude, you look like you need to get laid," he says, as he stirs sugar into his cup.

"Gee thanks."

"No, I mean it."

"I can tell. Also, who doesn't need to get laid?" I say, since, well, facts are facts. Grant shakes his head and just smiles like I'm not quite getting it. "It's not a philosophical question, man. It's more like words to live by."

"You flew across the country to give me this advice?" I joke, then take a drink too quickly. The coffee burns my tongue.

Great. Just great.

"No, I flew here because my guy and I are going to a friend's wedding before spring training. You just get this advice for free because I'm helpful like that," he says with a wink. "Bottom line is this—you need to just fuck Chris. Get him out of your system once and for all."

The ease with which he says it amazes me. First, because Grant isn't a casual guy either when it comes to relationships. Second, because . . .

"And then I'll see him again," I say. "He *is* in the same city, you know. Oh, yeah, we also happen to work in the same field and all. That'll be real fun when I play against him." I don't dare voice the part that weighs on me though—what if I want more and Chris doesn't?

"Look, I know you don't want a relationship after Harrison," Grant says carefully, reading my thoughts.

I fell hard for the Wall Streeter more than a year ago. We're talking hook, line, and sinker. We were together during the last off-season. Or I thought we were a thing. He thought we were just having a good time. Turned out, I was reading his signs all wrong.

So, yeah, I just don't want to go there again. The only saving grace after that bitter breakup was baseball. It saved my sorry ass from moping too much when he broke it off.

Baseball's all I need. Sure, the game breaks your heart. But it always gives you another chance.

"I'm thirty. I'm over hookups. I want to be someone's priority," I say, and it wasn't always easy to say those words.

For a long time, one-night stands were fun. But sometime in my late twenties, *fun* turned to *fine* turned to wanting something more. "I want something serious, and clearly, he's not serious."

"Dude. *Dude.* You don't know that he doesn't want the same thing. Did you try, you know, asking Chris?"

Not sure I need to ask him. He made it clear what he wanted in September outside the clubhouse. He made it clear again in October in the parking lot. Sure, I want to see him spread out and panting on my bed, losing his mind as I work him over. But I'd want to see him in the morning too, and he doesn't seem like a relationship kind of guy.

It's easier to say no than to get hurt again. That's why I drove away from him the last time I saw him.

Asking him is not in the cards. I meet Grant's eyes. "When did you become the Yoda of healthy relationships?"

My friend gives me the smile of the recently married and very well laid. "Or you could just bang it out and get him out of your system." Then he winks.

I flip him the bird. "Fuck you, Blackwood."

"Fuck you too," he says, then takes off to meet his husband.

After I drain my cup, I toss it in the recycling bin at the shop, then head out, debating whether my agent, my teammates, or Grant is offering the worst advice for how to handle today.

But lust is best handled on a full stomach, so I reward myself with a restorative breakfast sandwich at my favorite place.

The thing about New Yorkers is most people have them all wrong. They're not rude; they're succinct. They're not impatient; they're efficient. And god knows, ask them for anything, and they'll give you unvarnished advice whether you want it or not.

I ask my bodega guy for a bacon, egg, and cheese. What I get is a "Shoulda gotten that tag down earlier."

At least it's baseball advice, not relationship advice. So there's that.

I ask a cabbie to take me to Chelsea. What I get is a comprehensive history of the woes and struggles of the New York Union baseball organization.

That's another reason—if things don't work out with Chris, and they won't, everyone in this city will sing me some variation on *shoulda dated a hockey player instead.*

When I reach the building on Eighth Avenue, I wait in the lobby for the security guard to call the studio to confirm I'm allowed up. I don't tell him my name, but he says, "Yes, *that* Josh Spencer," in a tone like

I'm going to get an earful about the World Series.

It does buy me a few seconds where I don't have to see Chris. And remember that kiss against my car, the feel of his mouth on my neck. The way I almost said yes to his teasing. To toasting my own World Series defeat. To letting him slip under all my carefully built defenses.

Instead, the guard passes me the visitors' logbook. "Sign here, sir." And I autograph the visitors' book.

I slide it back to him. He chews his lip for a second, and I brace myself for whatever is coming my way—a rant, advice, or, worse, sympathy.

"I'm not supposed to ask, but can I get a picture?" he says.

"Sure, man." I duck down a little to get us both in the frame as he snaps a few.

"Great year last year."

"Even if it didn't end how we wanted it."

"Buck up. There's always next season." The guard gives me an optimistic twitch of his graying mustache.

I can't help but smile. "Yeah, I guess there is." And I promise that I'll do my best, then I find the bank of elevators.

Our teams arranged this publicity photoshoot, timed for the start of spring training. "It'll be a totally quick one-and-done thing, easy-peasy, don't even need to bring anything," Maritza said, when she asked me to do this for the Union. "Something to show there's no bad blood between you two now that baseball is back."

That's the message I've gotten since the end of October. *Play nice.* Like I'm the one who started it.

I stab the elevator button, then make my way up to the ninth floor. Will Chris be here already? Or will I have to wait for him? And why do I care?

Because I do.

When I exit the elevator and stride into the sleek, bright, white studio space, the answer is that he beat me here too.

And he looks so damn good that Grant's words push to the front of my mind. That I don't know if Chris wants the same thing. But I sure as hell know what I want, and he's currently lying on the studio's black leather couch, already charming the production assistant, a petite blonde with purple streaks in her hair.

"As long as you're not secretly a Boston fan, I can score you tickets anytime," Chris says.

Well, so can I. I hate Boston too.

But I keep that to myself, opting instead for a quick, "Hey there."

"Oh, good, the fun's arrived," he says.

Because that's what this is supposed to be. *Fun*.

5

JOSH

The production assistant aims a smile at me that's mostly teeth. "Yay, let's get started. You both can go get jerseyed up."

We're ushered over to a corner studio with a numeral six on the door; it has a makeshift dressing area to change in.

Together.

She leaves, shutting the door behind us.

Grant's words echo in my head. *Get it out of your system.*

Which is not helpful in studio sex.

I mean, six.

"This'll be fun," Chris deadpans.

"What'll be fun?" I ask cautiously.

"Pretending we like each other," he says, then winks, like I was pretty sure he did when he crossed home plate in the last game.

"I bet we can manage faking it," I say, since he can't always be the one with the smart-ass comments.

We stare at each other for a moment, my mind filled with all the shower thoughts I've had about him over the past few months. All the arguments, insults, recriminations. And maybe a few of the other things too, all of which are probably playing out in IMAX on my face.

"You should take off your pants," Chris says.

Did he just say that? "Excuse me?"

"We're supposed to get changed." He motions to a low table with our uniforms and gloves on it. "You look like you need some directions. So I thought I'd help you out."

I recover quickly, since I've got to hold my own against him. "You are so full of great advice," I say, as I discard my puffer coat on the table perhaps with a little too much force. "Can I give you some?" Though my advice would be for him to quit looking at me like that. Mostly, so I stop looking back.

"Nope," Chris says. "Can't improve on perfection. But since I'm feeling generous, this is how you're supposed to remove a shirt." He reaches for the back of his tee, slowly peeling it up, revealing the cut of his abs and the scattering of hair on his chest. I'm used to changing in front of guys, and having them change in front of me, but this is different. Especially when he gives that trademark grin of his. The one he's about to dazzle a camera with. The one that shouldn't work on me, but hell, it does.

Chris tosses his shirt on a nearby table. And then undoes his belt buckle.

It's loud in the otherwise empty space, the only other noise is the murmur of the crew as they set up. A reminder that I need to keep a level head for this photoshoot. Even if it feels impossible with him standing there, slowly easing the leather of his belt out of its loops then undoing his fly.

He taps his foot with mock impatience. "Now you."

A heavy World Series ring glints on his finger. It's somehow more obscene than if he were naked, the line of hair between his navel and the opened vee of his pants like a blinking arrow. Maybe my agent is right about this as an experience. Because I want to lean into not only our rivalry but also Chris over the couch.

He makes a little motion with his hand. I roll my eyes and try to take my shirt off with as little fuss as possible.

It doesn't help that he whistles.

I turn around, so my arousal isn't totally obvious. If that's possible. Then I finish changing, putting on the uniform pants, and leaving my jeans on the table. When I'm done, I get a cup of orange juice from the catering spread on the other side of the studio, and that cools me off.

So does the presence of the photographer. A Black woman with a swirl of tattoos and a heavy professional camera walks into the studio; she tells us her name is Sadie. The photoshoot is the kind I've done a hundred times before. We're in uniform, told to look charming at the camera. Chris looks charismatic. I probably look like I'm trying to fry the camera lens with my mind.

"Now stand back-to-back," Sadie says. I turn, focusing on a blank spot on the far wall. And not on the feel of Chris's back against mine.

We're standing close, though she encourages us closer, to narrow the thin humming strip of air between us.

"Act like you like each other," she says drily, since she obviously knows the score.

"We don't," I say, just as Chris says, "We do."

Maritza's instructions flash in my head. *Play nice.* I sigh. And inch closer.

Chris moves his hand behind his back and like that, our palms brush briefly, just enough to scrape the band of his championship ring against my fingers like he's making a point.

"Is that a fake ring?" I whisper. The team won't hand out the real ones until the beginning of this season.

"Why?" Chris's voice is a purr against my back. "You wanna try it on?"

A deliberate goad, and I won't let him have the last word, but firing off a comeback to that one is gonna be tough—a ring is only what I want most in the world. So I say nothing, just borrow a page from his playbook. *Touch.* I brush the tip of my finger along his, and a low, barely audible gasp escapes him. I just grin, pleased that I turned the tables for once.

And maybe turned him on too.

Fair play and all.

The move works on other levels since the photographer calls out, "Great, that's great. Way to bring the energy, Josh."

She takes us through more poses. Chris in his batting stance looking teasingly at the camera. Me miming like I'm snagging I throw from a catcher.

And of course, she wants us to reenact The Slide.

Because that was the other part of Maritza's instructions. I have to put on my best public relations smile and pretend like losing the World Series was no big deal. Because it's all good, clean fun. A *game*. Even if it means reliving one of the worst moments of my career.

The photographer is ready for this do-over. In a corner of the studio, there's a base set up, an infielder's glove for me to use as a prop. During the game, the slide itself took no more than a few seconds. Now, Sadie tells Chris to mimic his slide into my ankle.

Chris drops down, slowly, to his knees, and he flashes a smile up at me that's a reminder of how we last parted. How I spent the night I lost the World Series alone, half wishing I'd had the guts to say yes to him.

"Now get onto your side," she instructs, and Chris does, but not before gazing up at me with those blue eyes. And licking his lips.

"Like this?" he asks innocently, already draping himself not-so-innocently on the floor. His pants pull tight. His jersey hugs his chest. This guy can make anything arousing, including a reenacted slide.

He's unfairly sexy.

"Good, good," Sadie says. "Now Josh, tag him like you normally would."

The glove feels strange on my hand. I cannot for the life of me remember where I tried to tag Chris that night. On his calf? His knee? His back?

I brush the fingers of my glove along his outer thigh. Most players drop weight during the season and recover in the off-season. Chris has put it back on in muscle, and his legs test the confines of his gray uniform pants. They look good on him. Better if they were on my apartment floor.

"Little higher," he whispers, and shifts slightly, so I'm practically leaning over him, my glove against his ass.

But not quite, since of course I didn't get the tag down.

"Nice," she says. "Closer if you can. Josh, lean over him more. You want the impression of movement without actually moving."

"That's not realistic," I protest. The photographer shoots me a look. Right. This is about convincing the public I'm not a sore loser.

I lower myself farther so that my glove is

almost to his waist, and we're touching, his calf pressed to my thigh. The heat from his body radiates into the already-warm space. Chris must have shaved this morning, but there's the faint tinge of stubble along his jaw. It'd be slightly rough if I reached out and ran my hand down his face. Or if he rubbed his cheek against my thighs.

And that's not where my head should be going.

For one particular reason.

Yes, we're in our uniforms, except for one minor difference that makes a huge difference. No protective cups. Any effect he has on me will be obvious. And immortalized on a photographer's camera. I'm already halfway to broadcasting my lust to the three of us.

My hand shakes, shifting my glove slightly to tap it against Chris's ass.

"That tickles," he says.

"Sorry." I withdraw my hand.

"I don't mind," he says as if butter wouldn't melt on his tongue.

Distantly, my brain registers the click of the camera's shutter. It might as well be in outer space, the two of us in a bubble.

I don't think too much in this bubble. Just for once with him, maybe because I need to get *something* out of my system, I go for the stark truth. "I don't mind either," I say, low, just for Chris.

His bright blue eyes flicker with surprise, like they're saying *I didn't know you had that in you*.

The assistant steps in and says she needs Sadie for just a sec, and of course Chris takes advantage of the distraction. "Ohhh. Did you decide to be nice to me?" he asks.

"No," I say to Chris when Sadie leaves. Though it's hard to keep up a glare when I can feel the vibration of his laughter—when he knows I'm lying. Most of all, when it's just the two of us now.

"Too bad," Chris says. "Thought you might have reconsidered."

"Playing nice?"

"That. Maybe my other suggestions as well."

Lean into the rivalry. Get it out of my system. It'll be good to see Chris in controlled circumstances.

All that advice echoes in my mind.

In the end though, I listen to my gut.

It's now or never.

"Maybe I did." My throat goes dry. I considered that offer repeatedly and at great length over the past three and a half months. What he'd be like, out of his clothes and in my bed. If he'd still be as cocky. Some part of me wants to see him panting, wrung out, pleading. Another part wants to see him the next morning, drinking coffee with his hair sticking up in every direction.

I want all those things.

I don't say anything, but up close, my face doesn't keep any secrets.

Chris smirks. "You were thinking about me."

I give him my best bluff. "Only because the press won't stop asking me about you."

"Uh-huh. I'm sure that's it."

And I'm sure I'm done with games. Done with rules. And done with flirting. "Maybe I don't want to play nice," I say, then go for it. "Maybe I want you to show me how to play dirty after all."

His eyes are flames.

The door squeaks. Sadie is back and she clears her throat. "Sorry, guys, I need to take a call real quick. Should be less than ten minutes. Are you good keeping yourselves entertained?"

"We'll be fine," Chris says, in his best *nice guy* voice. "Take all the time you need."

6

CHRIS

Sadie closes the door on her way out, leaving Josh, me, and no room for any more excuses.

This is the opportunity I've been angling for.

This is what I want with Josh Spencer. Him wanting me with the same intensity. Him bending closer to me.

They've partitioned the room into various sets, two backdrops on either side of us, walling us from the rest of the room. I'm still stretched out, foot tagging a simulated base.

Even without a jock, the shorts I have on —the same kind we wear during games—are *confining*. Especially when I've been fighting getting a hard-on for the past ten minutes. Or really, since Josh walked in and scowled at me.

Maybe I have a fetish for derisive second basemen. Or one very specific second baseman. It helps that he's clearly been trying to keep himself under that famous Spencer control for the entire photoshoot. But the signs were there all along today, and yes, I have catalogued them. The slight shake in his hands. The sheen of sweat on his top lip that I want to lick off. His asking to play dirty.

I roll up slowly, like Josh might spook, before rising to my knees. I cup my dick like I would if I were adjusting myself during a game. Except of course, Josh is watching me.

I don't ask him if he likes what he sees. It's clear he does and whatever issues he's been hung up on for months don't have anything to do with the heat between us. For now, that's enough.

I give him a blink, an obvious tilt of my mouth, a second to tell me to stop. Then I wrap Josh's hand on the back of my neck and lean forward.

There's something to be said for being direct.

It takes me one second to get his belt buckle open, one more to undo the fly of his pants. He's in the same kind of shorts, visibly hard, straining. They're dark but I imagine the beginning of a wet patch on the fabric. I breathe on his stomach to watch the faint flutter of muscles and hair, and get rewarded with a gasp.

I look up at Josh through my eyelashes. "Sorry, did you want something?"

He grips the back of my neck.

I don't give him the satisfaction of giving in. "Last time I saw you, you were running your mouth about me. If you want something, you gotta ask for it."

"You know what I want," he bites out.

"Do I though? Maybe you should just make it crystal clear. After all, we've got ten minutes and counting."

His gorgeous brown eyes flash hot. And that's something to tuck away for later. If there's a later beyond my knees on the hard studio floors and the fact that he so clearly wants to fuck my face.

"Get your mouth on me," Josh says. And then adds, a little desperately, "Please."

Or maybe a lot desperately. "Oh you can have manners. Remember that the next time you mention me to the press," I say.

I kiss him, on his hip, through the fabric of his shorts. "Is that what you meant?"

"*Chris.* Give me something. Anything. Fuck."

I want to hear him say my name like that

again. Repeatedly. Possibly with his fingers threaded through the slats in my headboard. I'll settle for them threaded through my hair.

I peel down his shorts, revealing his cock. And yeah, wow. I guess that's why commentators say he swings a big bat.

Josh doesn't say anything else, but he doesn't need to after that magnificent beg. I lick him, a hot stripe up from his base to the head, and he makes a tiny fraction of a noise. A victory, one I relish in when I do it again, slow and indulgent. His hands grip my hair tighter. "We don't have a lot of time."

"We're not gonna need a lot." And then I suck him, taking him deep into my mouth, enjoying the slow dirty slide of his dick hitting my throat. It's fucking hot, and I shove my hand down my pants, working myself to the same rhythm. We go on like that for a minute, the world spun down to the weight of him in my mouth and his increasingly desperate panting. Which is good. Because it's not a competition for who can make the other come faster, but I'm definitely going to win.

Eventually, Josh tugs back on my hair. "Wait, wait."

I pull off. "You good?"

"So good." Above me, his face is flushed,

color up in his cheeks. His lips are red like he's been biting them, maybe trying to keep quiet. He looks hot, though a little too together, considering I feel like I'm going to pop any second. "Don't come yet," Josh warns. His voice sounds hoarse, the way my throat already feels. "I want to watch you."

Except that has the opposite effect from cooling me down, enough that I grip myself.

The couch is a few feet away. "We should —" I nod to it, and he manages himself over there, gripping his opened pants, before he flops back on the cushions. I sink to my knees again between his thighs, but he pulls me up, on top of him, the two of us a little too large for the couch.

We slide against each other, his chest solid against mine, his arms wrapped around me. His eyes are more vulnerable than I've seen before. "Can I kiss you?" he asks, and fuck, he looks so sweet that I have to.

The kiss starts off slow, a press of his mouth, the first pressure of his tongue, and we only have ten minutes, less than that. I want to get back to sucking him, but I don't want to stop kissing.

I want more than what the next ten minutes can provide.

I bite his lips, and he counters, deepening

the kiss, urging his fingers into my back, not speeding up, and we make out like that, in a slow, deliberate grind.

"Josh, we need to hurry." He shivers as I say his name. I want to feel it again. Today. Tomorrow. When we have time and a door that locks. If he still wants me after today. Or if this is just his way of getting me out of his system before the season starts. It wouldn't be the first time a guy's done that to me.

He shoves at the waistband of my pants, and I kick them down, pulling his along too, until we're pressed together, chest-to-chest and thigh-to-thigh.

"Here." He cups his palm, spitting into it, getting a hand between us, then kissing me again. He kisses like he wants to prove a point, and I kiss him right back and buck into his hand. I'm not worried about time now. I'm not worried about anything, not when he kisses like he's trying to lay claim over my mouth.

But Josh apparently is. "This is gonna be a mess," he gasps.

"I can fix that," I say.

There's enough space on the couch that I can scoot back, until I get my mouth on his dick again. This feels closer than we were before, me between his legs, my arm draped across his hips. His hand curls around my head, his fingers roping through my hair. A long, muffled moan comes next, then a full body shudder, and he finishes that way in my mouth. I pull off, licking him once as a tease, eliciting a gasped *Chris* that I want to bottle, save, store for the long season ahead.

I also want to come right this second.

Josh props himself up, looking at me, face flushed, mouth wet. There's no way the photographer won't know something's up. But I'm okay with that. Better than okay. So good with it I want to take out a billboard in Times Square that says, *Yeah, I made Josh Spencer come, and yeah, he called my name.*

I lift myself up to sit on my knees, leaning over him.

Josh reaches up with one arm, rubbing a thumb over the seam of my lips. His shirt is rucked up, revealing his chest and stomach. "Come on my chest. All over me," he commands.

And *fuck*, it doesn't take much, just a few cycles of my hand, and I'm doing just what he said, painting his skin with my release.

I collapse forward, panting, and the world goes pleasantly, amazingly blank.

After a minute, Josh taps me on the arm in an effort to get up. I roll off him, slumping against the back of the couch. Whatever mess Josh was hoping to avoid clearly didn't work. My pants are still open, and I reconcile myself to trying to get cleaned up when Josh comes back with a bottle of water from the catering spread, along with a handful of napkins. He's dabbing at his belly, frowning.

"Hey," I croak at him, and hell, my voice really is shot. If we do pre-season interviews, I'm going to have to cite a reaction to Florida pollen and not the Union second baseman's cock deep in my throat.

Josh smiles at me, the kind he doesn't give when he's pretending to like the press, but a real one, soft at the edges.

"Here." He hands me the bottle of water, which I drain, then follows it up with the napkins, swiping them over my stomach.

Eventually, reality sets in. I stand, straightening up further, trying to look like we haven't been doing exactly what we've been doing. Except every so often, Josh shoots me a look like he can't believe that happened either.

Noises drift closer from outside the studio, the crew returning. We look decent enough, even though my lips are stinging from the scrape of his beard and my hair a mess.

Josh's jersey is back on, but he skipped a button. I reach out, sliding it into the button-hole, feeling the firmness of his chest underneath it, wondering what's next. If we'll part ways to go to Florida for six weeks of meaningless scrimmage games before the season starts. That once he's had the Chris Garnett experience, he'll decide it's not for him.

Josh drops his gaze to my hands on his shirt, watching me as I finish dressing him. I can feel his heart thumping fast.

He lifts his face, his expression maybe like he's working through something, solving a problem. "Come get a drink with me," Josh says. "After this."

I pretend to consider it, so I don't sound overeager. "Well, I don't know. It's noon, and I'm flying to Miami later today."

"Coffee, then. A mimosa. A glass of water. I don't care." Josh is so intense, asking me just like he plays ball.

Warmth blooms in my chest. "Careful, Spencer. If you keep that up, someone might think you like me." I hope he does, and it's not just the spectacular orgasms talking.

Josh starts to say something when the photographer returns, shaking her head. "Sorry about that, guys. I didn't mean to be gone so long."

"It wasn't an issue," I say to Sadie. "That's the thing about baseball. There's a lot of hurry up and wait, so you always find a way to keep entertained."

Behind me, Josh coughs like he's trying not to laugh. I head to the table, getting two more little bottles of water, and handing him one.

"You sound like you're thirsty," I say. Josh gives me a flat look, so clearly, I have to keep going. Winding him up is so much fun. "You might want to watch that. I can feel a sore throat coming on. Must be the weather."

"I'll be sure to invest in some tea," he says. Though it sounds like he wants to give me another sore throat, possibly as soon as we get out of here. "Maybe I'll get some after this. If you . . . want to get some too."

I smile at that, a real smile that he answers with one of his own. "Sure, I'd be happy to come with you."

7

CHRIS

After the photoshoot, we quickly change back into our street clothes. Or, really, Josh changes quickly and I stare shamelessly as he tugs on his shirt and jeans. He has to hop to get on the latter—mostly because his thighs look like pre-spring training tree trunks—and actually laughs about it. As much as I want to see this man naked, his rush to get out of here is somehow hotter.

Like he can't wait to buy me a glass of the city's finest tap water.

Funny, but I can't wait either.

But when we reach the sidewalk, Josh shoves his hands in his pockets, some of that eagerness vanishing. The streets are coated in February slush; I'm so ready to head to Florida and start the season. Or to see Josh shirtless on a beach, covered in sunscreen and Florida sand.

"You don't have to get a drink if you don't want to," he says.

A one-eighty from how he was upstairs, but maybe that's the endorphins wearing off. Maybe out here in the real world, he's regretting . . . *something*. I smile because anything else will give away my disappointment. Still, I want him to know the score. "I don't say yes to things I don't want to do," I say, eyes locked with his.

Josh's face goes through a series of expressions that land on *pleased*. "I looked up a couple places around here while you were getting changed."

"Not watching me?"

"I can multitask."

"Noted." We're standing under the awning at the entrance, which is lined with heaters to melt away the snow. It's warm, but even so, Josh blushes further, a pink tinge to his cheeks that makes me want to kiss him again. Right here. I restrain myself and ask, "Where'd you find?"

"Did you want a beer or a cup of coffee? Or . . . there's a bunch of places that do fancy tea. If your throat is still sore."

That makes it my turn to blush, only

slightly—not at what he said, but at the memory of minutes ago. Of the way he gasped and came down my throat, how he tasted on my tongue, and the soft look in his eyes after. "Your dick's not that big, Spencer," I tease.

Josh shrugs at that, looking smug, like he's daring me to press the point. "So no tea?"

"I'll take a drink. If you're offering." I check the time on my phone. "Though, fair warning, I've got a plane to catch later today."

His pleased expression fades slightly.

"So," I add, "you're gonna have to romance me real fast." I wink for good measure.

He laughs. "Just because you're fast on the base paths doesn't mean you have to be fast everywhere else. Like, say, back at the studio."

"I didn't hear you complaining about a damn thing back there," I tease, though it occurs to me that at some point I ought to make it clear what I mean by *romance me.* Maybe sooner rather than later.

We end up at a place in Hell's Kitchen. It's early enough in the day that the server deposits us in a booth in the back with ice waters, then tells us to order at the bar whenever we're ready. The place has the look of a refurbished speakeasy, exposed brick and a pressed tin ceiling. It's nice. Different from most of the places big-leaguers drink.

And this could be the moment for sooner. I drum my fingers on the table, then meet his eyes.

"Is this a date?" Because it feels like a date. Unless it's a goodbye.

Josh swallows a gulp of ice water. "It doesn't have to be."

"I didn't say I minded," I say, hoping that gets me closer to an answer. And him too.

"It can be whatever it is," he says, which doesn't clear things up either as to whether this is a real date or not.

But maybe that's not his thing? "When was the last time you went out with some-one?" I ask. "Like out-out. Not just a hookup."

"My ex and I broke up before the season last year. So it's been a while since I went out with anyone seriously."

Said with the possible implication that I'm not. "Wow, you really are a baseball monk. No one since then?"

"No one real serious." Josh rotates the ice in his glass. "How about you?"

"It's been a while."

His eyes widen. "Really?"

"Yes. Really," I say, with emphasis.

He hums. Maybe scoffs.

"This shocks you?"

"I mean, when you look like"—he gestures at my face—"and I'm sure the World Series ring didn't hurt. You could have whoever you want."

"And yet, I'm sitting here with you," I say, never breaking my gaze, letting the answer land. One more step toward clarity with this guy who can be hard to read.

Josh smiles at that, a slow spread of a smile, different from the others I've seen. "Well, this is a nice table and all, so a good place to be sitting," he says drily.

I laugh. "A very good place. You really want to know what I did for most of November?"

He stares at me sharply. "You wanna rub it in that we lost? *Again*?"

"Nah. I told you I'd be gentle if you want me to. Anyway, I partied, sure, but mostly I slept and did TV spots. And, you know, there was this guy who plays for the New York Union who, every time I turned on The Sports Network, there he was, being asked about me. I think he might have called me a dirty player once or twice."

"Once," he corrects. "The night of the game. And I never actually said *dirty*."

"Uh huh."

"I didn't."

"You sure didn't correct the media when they implied it, though."

Josh's face turns serious and he sighs. "You're right, I didn't. I was running pretty hot the night we lost. I probably said some things I shouldn't have."

There's a napkin on the table, wicking up condensation from his drink. He runs his finger over the edge of it. He exhales, like he's gearing up for something, then meets my eyes. "I was reeling from the loss. And the possibility that maybe I missed my chance with you," Josh says it quietly, biting his lip.

His eyelashes are a dark shadow on his cheek. And his admission makes me think that yes this is a real date. And I have that much of an answer to at least that one question.

"You didn't, Josh," I say. "Miss it, I mean."

Josh smiles, grabs a menu, and hands it to me. "Pick a drink. I'll go order."

"Oh, you're that kind of boyfriend," I tease.

His smile falters.

"It was a joke." Of course it was. Because that's my luck. Most of the guys I think of as potential boyfriends only end up as the suffix.

Friends. I reach out, scanning the menu. "I'll take a martini. A dirty one."

Josh heads to the bar, and I watch him, enjoying the view. He returns a few minutes later with two drinks, a beer and a cocktail glass he slides toward me.

"The bartender assures me this is quote-unquote extra dirty," he says.

"Perfect for me, then."

"Yes, it has your name all over it, Chris," Josh says as he rolls his eyes. He lifts his beer but stills when I wave my hand to stop him.

"No toast?" I ask.

"What are we drinking to?"

I tap my championship ring against the glass. "The World Series?"

Josh shakes his head a little despairingly. "Anything but that."

"Second dates?" I offer, hopeful he'll see this the same way.

His mouth has an amused tug to it and that looks good on him. "How about third ones?"

That's even better. "Ambitious." We touch glasses, and I drink. "This is really excessively dirty."

"I can get you another one." He's halfway standing before I can object. So he really is that kind of boyfriend. Just not mine. Yet.

"It's fine. It's good." I drink more of it to prove my point, and he resettles. It's a curved booth, and he slides in closer so that we're thigh to thigh. "Besides," I add, "I think this *is* technically our third date."

"I don't think half-making out in a parking lot counts as a date."

"I meant the golf tournament. Even though you were all . . ." I make a look of mock intensity, frowning slightly and pursing my lips.

"Well, it was that or try not to stare at your ass in those golf pants. Who makes golf pants look that hot?"

"You didn't do a great job of hiding that because I caught you looking about seven times. Then three during lunch, but who's counting?"

"You obviously."

"Well, I'm into baseball analytics."

He cracks up. "I'll say."

"But also, you were so intense about the tournament and I think everyone else was kinda buzzed," I say.

He mumbles something into his glass about the sport.

"Didn't catch that," I say.

"I'm not very good at golf and I, uh, got lessons."

"For real?"

"It was for a children's charity. I didn't want to embarrass myself or not raise money or whatever."

And that's officially adorable. I kiss him, on the cheek, right at the edge of his beard. It scrapes pleasantly against my lips. He turns into the kiss until our lips brush. And he doesn't kiss with the same desperation he did back at the studio. This is a date kiss. A relationship kind of kiss and that's sort of terrifying and wonderful at the same time. A whole different kind of intensity, especially when I pull back. But he'll have none of that. He winds a hand around the back of my neck. Our foreheads touch.

And Josh doesn't stop. He returns to my lips with slow, decadent kisses. He's not in a rush at all. He just coasts his lips across mine, explores my mouth, and takes all the time in the world. His hand lingers on my thigh. His other hand plays with the ends of my hair, and holy hell. Josh Spencer can kiss, and my head is a haze. A dreamy, delicious fog of his scent and his want, and the utter strangeness of my life right now. The last time I saw him he walked away, and this time he's kissing me like he never wants to stop.

But I can't let my mind go there. To what

this might be. This is just an unexpected early afternoon drink. We're both leaving for spring training in mere hours. As much as this might feel like a *something more* kiss, things between two rivals who exchanged heated words don't change just like that. With a blow job, and a martini, and a stolen midday moment.

Eventually, Josh pulls back. "We should probably—" He nods to where a few more patrons have come in. No one glances our way, but New Yorkers have the habit of looking particularly unimpressed and snapping photos of you at the same time. We might end up on Page Six or, worse, Twitter.

Josh is out, so am I. But if we're dating, we're going to be the subject of every headline and breathless hot take. Which isn't what I'm looking for when I don't even know if Josh wants this to go beyond today. I take a few calming breaths, because the martini might be mostly olive, but that doesn't stop that feeling close to giddiness from creeping in. "So yeah, that tournament. I don't know. You were frowning, and checking my ass out and also texting someone."

"My ex. I left stuff at his place. When I got there, he opened a drawer of other people's shirts that he accumulated and just told me to take the ones that were mine."

"Ouch. No wonder you looked like a human rain delay."

His eyebrows go up in question.

I motion with my hand above my head. "You had a little storm cloud and everything."

He laughs at that, not an on-field Spencer laugh like when he swipes me out stealing, but a real genuine Josh laugh. "You want to know what I remember from that tournament? You kept goofing around—"

"Thanks."

"And still whupped everyone's ass at golf. I was kind of impressed."

"Only kind of?"

"Okay, so you were hot, and funny, and seemed like you were having a good time without taking everything so seriously, and if I wasn't in the process of being broken up with by someone who didn't think he was dating me, I probably would have asked you to get a drink that day."

Well, it's a whole new ballgame today with Josh. Something in him unlocked. And I want to keep turning the key.

I press my thigh against his, pushing against that muscular leg under the table. "I'd have said yes, Josh."

He dips his face, smiles a little shyly. It's so damn cute how he can go from being bold enough to order me to shoot all over his pecs to borderline bashful.

The more I learn about the secret mind of Josh Spencer, the more I want to get to know him both in bed and out of bed.

That also means I want to know why he put up a wall that night in September. "So tell me something. Why'd you say no the night I asked you to grab a beer? After the game. Outside your clubhouse."

Josh scoff-laughs. "You remember that? Every detail?"

Time for me to blow his mind. "I remember when guys I want turn me down."

"What do you know? I usually remember when hot, funny men ask me out. So I remember every detail too." Josh fiddles with the label on his beer then shrugs. "But it's probably different for you because you get it so often."

I stare hard at him like *gimme a break, Josh*. "On a first date," I correct, then I drain most of my martini, which tastes like olives and slightly warming gin. "Less frequently for the second."

He arches a skeptical brow. "This is in New York?"

"Yeah. Let's go with a not-insignificant portion of Manhattan."

"Huh. Didn't realize that there were that many stupid guys on this island."

"Well, technically you'd be one of them, *Josh*," I say, taking my time with his name, enjoying the feel of it. The possibility of saying it another day, then another. Enjoying too the images playing out in my head right now. The things I want to do to him. "If I weren't getting on a plane in a few hours . . ."

He gives me a slow smile. "Yeah?"

I nod, slow and long, making my meaning clear. "The things we could do."

"Bet I'd like those things."

"Bet we both would," I rasp out. "As long as you're not so stupid the next time I ask you to go home with me."

That smile he keeps flashing my way is full of all sorts of promise. "Well, sometimes, I can be pretty fucking stupid. But I'm working on it."

8

JOSH

I'm also working on what's next for me.

What's next for him is a flight to Florida. Chris is going to be out that door in five minutes. Maybe this is my one shot with him. But do I just say *Hey, you want to do this again? And maybe again*? I don't entirely have the best track record of consistency with Chris, but then I don't know if he does either when it comes to the stuff I want—to be important to someone. To matter.

I want to be the guy someone depends on, and I want someone to rely on me. I also want to get him naked for a good long while.

As I search his cool blue eyes for an answer to all my own questions, I desperately want the answer to be . . . him and me.

But I only have a chance of getting that if I have the guts to ask a big question.

I gear up for it, working through options in my head. *Want to meet on an off day during spring training?*

But that sounds like too much too soon.

Want to do this again in six weeks?

And that feels like I'm planning too far ahead.

Chris Garnett isn't known for that.

He's the *just for fun* guy. He's the guy who wants to get me in bed. Out of it—who knows?

But, hell, I like the man. More than I expected. More than I'm prepared to. And I wish I could be as fearless in romance as I am at the plate.

Maybe I can try though. Take a step toward him.

"So, what do you think about maybe playing pool sometime?" I ask, figuring I'll use his words from that September game when he asked me to play.

"Holy shit. It's Spencer and Garnett!"

I cringe.

I jerk my gaze away from Chris, and into the eyes of a big dude with a big booming voice and a thick Queens accent. He's not alone. The guy's got an entourage with him. Four other dudes, in baseball jerseys, a mix of Gothams and Union. The big dude points from Chris to me. "I thought you guys hated each other. Did you, like, make up?"

The back of my neck prickles. Shit. Did they see us conducting a kissing clinic a few minutes ago? That's not exactly how I wanted to go public with my, ahem, change of heart about my rival.

The last thing I want is for the whole damn city to know I've got it bad for him, only for him to walk away.

My jaw ticks, and I try to summon up a PR perfect answer. But none comes.

Chris laughs easily, then fires up that smile, clapping me on the shoulder, bro-dude style. "We're working on it. We've been debating how far the Knicks are going this year, but it seems we disagree on that."

"But you guys are, like, hanging. That's awesome. Putting the bad blood behind you," another fan says.

Yeah, I'd say we did that.

In the studio.

On the couch.

Here in this booth.

Chris turns his smile to me, all laidback and casual, the guy who flirted with me incessantly throughout the season. The guy who just ... flirts.

"We did. And now we're friends," he says.

My shoulders tense. Friends? But then I talk myself down. He's not going to tell a fan what we are. But what the hell are we? "Yup, we're friends," I say, so I don't come across as uncomfortable as I feel.

"Can we get a pic?"

And the last five minutes of my first real date with Chris Garnett turn into a selfie session with a bunch of guys from Queens. By all counts, this is good. I've wanted this since I was a kid. To play the game at the highest level, to have fans.

But all I want right now is to snag a minute alone with Chris.

Only as these guys take pic after pic, the minutes tick away.

And it's time for me to settle the tab. I say goodbye to the fans, head to the bar, pay the bill, and meet Chris on the street.

A glance at his watch tells me this stolen moment is over.

"So," he says, tucking his thumbs into his jeans pockets. "I guess when they tag us on Twitter and Insta, everyone will know we cleared the air."

"Our teams will be so proud."

"Yeah, they'll be stoked we don't hate each other anymore."

"We'll be like Jeter and A-Rod. Buds," I say.

Now it's his turn to frown.

Then he seems to erase it, nods, and says, "Yeah, we're friends."

Chris grabs his phone. "Then, since we're *friends*, you should give me your number," he says.

As I give him mine, I take out my phone and save his name and number when he sends me a text.

I write back with **looking forward to seeing you on third base.**

When it lands on his phone, he raises an eyebrow before tapping something on the screen.

I wait, but a text doesn't appear.

"Just making a quick update to your contact display name," Chris says. "*Friend.*"

That's not what I wanted to be with Chris Garnett. But maybe it's a start. For now, though, it's time for him to take off, and for me to let him. "See you around," I say.

He claps me on the back, a ballplayer bro hug, and no one in this whole city could be the wiser that an hour ago my hands were in his hair, his lips were crushed to mine, and his kisses made me want all the things with him.

That scares the hell out of me so I let him go.

9

JOSH

In the backseat of the car, a few hours later, I fiddle with my phone. Typing and deleting. Trying to untangle this new knot of emotions for the third baseman I can't get out of my head.

This is so ridiculous. I had one date with the guy.

But was it really only one date?

It's kind of been . . . all season.

And he's kind of been on my mind for a long time.

But I feel like I struck out looking back there, and that's the worst way to go at the plate.

As the driver weaves through traffic on the way to the airport, I try to figure out what

I want to say to Chris. So I take some practice swings.

Josh: Hey.

Josh: Hey Chris.

Josh: Chris I hope your flight's going okay.

Josh: I'm sorry we left off like that. I wanted to tell you before you left that . . .

I stare at the screen. "Nice effort, Spencer," I mutter, shaking my head. I delete those half-hearted attempts. Time to step it up. I try one more time, taking a deep breath before I type out the stark truth.

Josh: I like you. A whole fucking lot. I'm so into you. It's kind of crazy. And I want to see you when we're back in New York. For a drink in Hell's Kitchen again. For a night at my place. For . . . both. And more than one date. Or two. I don't know who all these other guys are who didn't want to go out with you again,

but they're fools. Or I guess not, because now
we get a chance. If you want one.

There. I said it. And hell, I strangely feel
better. Maybe I needed to say it to myself first.
To put it all out there in black and white. To
know what I want. I start one more message,
but I stop.

Text is not the way I want to tell him I'm
into him. I'd rather say all this to his face. His
sexy, adorable, smoldering face I want to see
day after day.

I check the schedule. The Union play the
Gothams the day after I return from spring
training.

Normally I can't wait for the season to
start. But this year is even worse. Six long
weeks away from each other.

Hmmm. Not sure I can wait.

And kinda don't want to wait to tell Chris
how I feel till I return to New York. But the
chances of us seeing each other before then is
slim. We're both starters, so my team won't
send me four hours across the state to Miami.
Same for him the other way.

So, as we near the airport, I call in a solid

and ask Yoda. The guy should know what to do. He's married to another baseball player.

Josh: So, you were right.

Grant: Of course I'm right.

Grant: About what?

Josh: Me and that guy.

Grant: You banged it out! Yes!

Josh: Sort of.

Grant: Josh, are you confused about how banging works? Fine, I can explain the basics. First, get some top-shelf lube . . .

Josh: Yeah, I get that part, dickhead. That's not the issue. The real issue is—yes. You were right. Yes, I need to put myself out there. Yes, I want to see the guy. So . . . what's next?

But before he can reply, I know the answer.

I've known it since we parted ways on a chilly New York sidewalk.

Grant isn't the person I need to talk to. I need to talk to Chris.

10

CHRIS

The night I arrive in Florida, I'm sitting out on the deck at my rental place, definitely not staring at a blank text thread, when three dots pop up.

Josh: ...

Of course, sharing a rental place means that my teammates—my wonderful, talented teammates, who will forever be my brothers in a shared championship—are here. They're also world champ snoops.

"Wow, what'd *Josh* do to earn an eggplant

emoji?" our first baseman asks. "Or is that a rating scale and one eggplant is the lowest?"

"Nothing," I say. "It's an inside joke. We're just friends." Saying that feels approximately like swallowing sawdust. I wash my mouth out with a swig of ginger ale.

Eventually, the dots disappear. My disappointment doesn't.

* * *

The next day my phone pings. And I'm not so disappointed anymore when the eggplant emoji graces my screen.

Josh: How's Florida?

Chris: Aren't you also in Florida?

Josh: The Gulf Coast is totally different. Miami's fun.

Chris: Any place I am is fun :). Tampa can't be that bad.

Josh: Spring training, you know? They keep calling us the league champions. Like that'll make up for not being world champions.

Chris: Sorry not sorry.

Josh: Thanks for rubbing it in.

Chris: Happy to rub it in any time. At length. Great length.

Josh: I may have a vague recollection of . . . length.

Josh: You going out a lot?

Chris: Mostly hanging out and going to the beach. How about you? Or would it cut down on your brooding time?

Josh: Didn't figure you for a homebody.

Chris: Depends on whose home. And whose body.

Josh: Sounds like a good setup.

Chris: [picture of the Miami shoreline taken through the window. Chris's reflection is visible.]

Josh: Nice view.

Josh: The ocean.

Chris: Just the ocean?

Josh: Also not the ocean.

Josh: Sorry is this weird?

Chris: You flirting with me? Or you flirting with me when we're not on second base?

Josh: Sometimes it was on third.

I don't answer, not right away. Not because I don't want to. But because that *was* pulses in my mind. Josh said he was afraid he missed his opportunity. But maybe I missed mine, too afraid to take a chance and swing.

I'm staying with some teammates at a house near our spring training complex. Normally, I don't mind living with other people—I like the noise, the activity—but maybe I've gotten older or they've gotten louder because it turns out to be a mistake.

Because they're looking to party. And I'm looking to get my head right. And my heart.

I do what any grown man faced with

housemates who play electronica way, way, way too loud at all hours would do. I whine to a friend. In this case, Jamie DeLuca, who's a catcher with the Miami Swordfish.

I call him from the deck of my rental, as the music blasts painfully inside. "Can I come stay with you?"

"That'd be a pretty long commute," Jamie says. "But you can come hang out for a while."

So I drive down to his place, a luxury high-rise about forty minutes south. He buzzes me up right away. His pad turns out to be a nice-ass penthouse condo overlooking the beach. "Wow," I say, looking around, "Miami must be treating you well."

"I'm renting it. The landlord's pretty reasonable." He smirks like there's more to it than that. "I'll give you the full tour later."

We head into the living room, which is decorated within an inch of its life—maybe beyond that—bright enough that I try not to laugh. There's art, a lot of it, or what I think is art but could be random knickknacks.

"Who did you say owned this place?"

"Uh, Matt Mackenzie."

"Your landlord is *Matt Mackenzie*?"

Jamie grins. We've known each other for a long time, ever since Jamie was a minor leaguer with the Union, before he was traded to Miami. I've learned to recognize the categories of his grins, and this one is definitely an *I'm getting away with something* smile. In part because he's apparently renting from a guy everyone in the game calls Big Mack, who was once the franchise player for the Baltimore Oysters. Baseball pays me pretty well but Mack is loaded. And apparently he decided to spend his money on some very tacky decorations.

"How much did you say you were paying to live here?" I ask.

Jamie deflects. "Like I said, the rent is very reasonable." Which sounds like there's a story there, but maybe for another time.

He leads me around the place, showing off the various amenities, with a slightly incredulous look between *Rich people, amiright?* and that he can't believe he lucked out.

We end up in the living room. Jamie gestures to the vastly overstuffed couch. "Sit anywhere."

I collapse across one end while Jamie sits on the other.

"What has you ready to flee spring training already?" he asks.

"Nothing." Though I sound petulant.

"Oh, it's like that? Because you only sound like that if it's guy trouble or baseball trouble and you won the World freaking Series last year."

Which is a sore spot for him because he was traded away from the Union, who are actually competitive, to the Swordfish. Who are not.

"It's not guy trouble. I think you have to be something other than *good friends* for it to be trouble."

Jamie gives a slightly solemn nod. "That's the worst kind of trouble."

"What would you do in my situation?"

"I'd say talk about it with him, if you want."

"We did talk about it. We're *friends*." Friends who hooked up once. Like a lot of my friends, who were lousy first dates but better friends.

"Well, it sounds like there's nothing you can do to change your situation," he deadpans.

"Thank you for the sarcasm."

"Technically, I was being sardonic."

"All right, Mister Ivy League, whatever." I sit up straighter, run a hand through my hair. I need to figure shit out. So I ask him seriously, "What are my other options?"

He grabs an Xbox controller off the coffee table. "*Rocket League* is also a valid coping mechanism. There's also really good food delivery."

"See, I knew I could count on you."

We play for a while. Some of the tension winding up my bones since Josh and I parted ways on the sidewalk, starts to unspool. And as it slinks away, the options become clearer. Maybe more necessary too. Since, yeah, playing Xbox with Jamie when I'm not on the field is a good way to pass the time. But I want more than just entertainment.

And I want it with the guy on the other side of the state.

So, I should take a step toward Josh.

"I *could* call him," I say, more nonchalant than I feel. "Friends call each other?"

Jamie doesn't stop playing the game. "Sure, you called me, after all."

The fucker. He's baiting me. Jamie knows it's not the same with him. Obviously.

On-screen, my little cartoon car pushes an oversized soccer ball around. "We could probably make plans or something. For when I'm back in the city. Just as friends."

Lies I tell myself. But hey, if it gets me in the same room as Josh, I'll keep fibbing.

Another noise of agreement.

"Dinner even. But we both work kind of late. So it'd have to be a late dinner," I say, liking that idea.

"Of course."

"And I *should* definitely call ahead. Last time we went out for drinks, there were fans. And it's easier if we don't have to deal with that. If we can just ..."

Be alone together.

"That's only reasonable."

"Maybe there's a backroom at this restaurant," I add, as I score a goal and the ball explodes into a puff of graphical dust. That sounds brilliant too. A backroom, without any interfering press, or fans, or excuses.

"This all sounds like good planning."

I put the controller down, abandoning the game, then level him with a stare. "You're really not going to say anything? *Chris, that sure as shit sounds like a date to me.*"

Because a date is exactly what I just planned.

Correction: Another date.

A third date. A fourth. Until we stop counting dates and start counting months.

Jamie laughs. "I've never known you to be anything other than direct. I'm told that if you want something, you should go after it.

So, unless he's throwing up stop signs, why not?"

That's a valid question, so I run through the answers to it.

"He might say 'no.'"

"He might."

"It'd suck if he did."

"It probably would."

"But," I begin, and even though I don't like either of those two scenarios at all, the risk is worth it. I can't get Josh out of my head. No, I don't *want* to get him out of my head. "I won't know until I try."

"That is true. You won't know until you know," he says.

I picture Josh, his deep brown eyes, his intensity, his dry humor. Then, the moments of vulnerability and need—moments that drew me closer to him. When he asked on the couch if he could kiss me, when he asked me out for a drink, when he smiled at me at the bar and asked me to play pool before a bunch of fans came crashing in.

If only we found more time.

I guess that's what we have now, and for the next six weeks. That's the thing about time: It's always limited when you don't want it to be and infinite when you just want it to hurry the hell up.

"I should probably call him." I dig in my pocket for my phone.

Jamie, taking the hint, gets up from the couch.

"Sorry, didn't mean to evict you from your own living room."

"It's Mack's living room. And I'm good. I should go review game footage anyway."

"It's spring training."

"Never too early to be prepared. Take your time."

After Jamie leaves, I sit and study my phone, trying to formulate how to say, *date me, date me, date me* without actually saying that. Or at least using better words. Finally, I open up FaceTime, finger hovering over the icon to hit Call, when my phone starts buzzing.

Josh: *FaceTime Request*

I don't drop the phone answering it, mostly because I'm an All-Star third baseman with the reflexes of a professional athlete. Also, the couch cushions catch it. I look startled when I answer, and probably sound out of breath when I say, "What's up?"

But none of that matters when I see Josh.

"Hey," he says. He looks soft at the edges. His hair is in slight disarray. Something about it makes me wish I could climb through my phone screen and kiss him.

"You doing okay?" I ask.

"I managed to tweak my hammie during our first practice."

"Shit."

"It's not serious. I'm day-to-day." He does air quotes around day-to-day. "They might have given me a muscle relaxer."

That would explain the slightly blissful smile he aims at me.

"Someone there taking care of you?"

"I got—" He makes a vague hand gesture behind him. "Guys are bringing me food for dinner."

"Okay, good. Wouldn't want you to wither away." Even if he's wearing a T-shirt with the sleeves hacked off and I can see just how good he looks.

He also looks like he's half asleep, a suspicion that's confirmed when he yawns, then asks, "How's Miami?"

"It's good." I sit up a little so that the living room comes into view behind me on screen.

"You want a tour of a really ridiculous condo?"

He gives me a slightly sleepy smile, then nods. "I do."

I get up from the couch. I aim the phone camera at a shelf that appears to be full of glass vases.

Josh's eyes widen on screen. "What are those?"

"Probably a couple thousand bucks each."

Josh laughs at that. "Those are so, um, well, colorful? Where are you?"

"I'm hanging out at DeLuca's place. Those aren't his. He's staying with Big Mack if you can believe it."

"Wow, how is that dude? I worshipped him growing up."

"Haven't seen him yet other than his condo."

"Looks like a pretty nice setup."

And it is. Peaceful. Quiet. Enough to leave me alone with my thoughts, which are mostly about the guy who's smiling at me on my phone screen, fond creases around his eyes. "You wanna see the rest of the place?"

"Gimme the full tour."

I spend a few minutes showing him everything: More terrible art, the TV setup he grunts over, and the kitchen he actually has questions about.

"Wow, look at that vent," he says. "How many BTUs is the stove?"

"I didn't know you could cook."

A shrug, one I recognize from the Josh Spencer False Modesty collection. "Maybe. A little. I could cook for you sometime."

Which sounds like something more than friends but not a conversation we should have while he's a little doped up.

Even though, yes, I want him to cook for me.

We talk for a while, mostly about spring training, but also about stuff I didn't know about him. That he grew up near Baltimore. That he sometimes bats barehanded for all of spring to toughen his hands. That he sponsors a youth league team in Dundalk and plays in a game with them every year. I tell him I'm from Petaluma, an hour north of San Francisco, and he says that tracks, me being from California. Petaluma's not far from wine country, and that perks his interest. I file that away too, the idea that we could go there someday. Eventually he yawns, long and lasting. He looks cozy under a throw blanket. It's a four-hour drive from Miami to Tampa; I know because I've Google Map'd it a bunch of times. But seeing him like this makes me want to say screw it and jump in my truck. Except, friends don't drive clear across Florida just because a *friend* has a slightly tweaked hamstring.

Maybe that's exactly why I should offer.

"I should let you go," I say, but I'm smiling at him, and saying it like I don't mean it as I settle back onto the couch.

"But you're not going to?" he asks, in the same tone, and it makes my heart hammer.

Josh snuggles deeper into the blanket, and it's a good thing his eyes are drifting closed, because I don't know what my face is doing right now.

"Maybe not quite yet," I say.

"Good," he says, almost like he's humming. Maybe with the same damn hope? "Thank you," Josh adds.

"For what?"

"I wasn't sure you were gonna pick up when I called."

"Of course I'd pick up," I say.

"Just with the way we left things . . ." Another yawn, and clearly he's losing whatever battle against sleep, though not entirely. Since he seems to fight to keep his eyes open as he murmurs, "I miss you."

Those are the best words ever. "I miss you

too," I say, then I seize the chance. I don't want to be just friends with Josh Spencer. "I haven't been able to stop thinking about you."

Josh's eyes open wide. "Yeah, I didn't think you were stupid either."

"Only about you."

That grin returns, only it feels like a brand-new kind, one made just for me. "I don't know if I can drive with my hammie like this," he says.

Wait. Is he talking about work now? I give him a look because maybe the meds are making him a little groggy. "Is someone gonna take you to the park?"

"I meant to come see you. So you're gonna have to come see me," he says, like a declaration.

And it's not the meds talking at all. Still, I kind of can't believe my luck. "You really can't wait to see me?" Though I'm already mentally running through our schedule, wondering if I can talk the coaching staff into putting me on the roster for our games in Tampa. Which they've already said no to. Twice. Yes, I've been angling for a chance to see this guy.

"I can't." Josh says it simply, but it makes my heart do something in my chest similar to when we won the World Series. A champagne celebration. A ticker tape parade.

"I can't either," I admit.

We sit there for a second, just smiling at each other, until Josh shifts how he's holding the phone, wincing.

"Leg hurt?"

"It's not great."

"You gonna take it easy? Gotta make sure you're ready for the season."

"You really want another go against us?"

"The last one didn't turn out too bad for me." I wave my hand, even though it's missing the replica championship ring I was wearing the last time we saw one another.

"Yeah, yeah, rub it in." But he's smiling. "See if you can make it out here. And if not in Florida, I think we might have something scheduled right at the beginning of the season."

Because of course we're playing against each other for our first game. "It's a date," I say, and I can't wait for it.

"Count on it."

11

CHRIS

Two Weeks Later

There are some days you dream of as a kid in your backyard. Hitting a mammoth home run, winning a championship, sitting atop a float at a victory parade as the city screams your name.

But there are others you don't know to dream about. Like how satisfying it is to get booed by a ballpark's worth of spring training fans as you're announced at a meaningless game in mid-March.

The ballpark only holds ten thousand people, but they're all Union loyalists and loud in their disappointment that their team lost the World Series. An especially boisterous chorus of boos greets me as I swing over the railing, jogging out to take my position at third base. The noise intensifies, though I cup my hand to my ear as if I can't hear them. That only aggravates them further. I smile, because the love and adulation of the home crowd is one thing, but a ballpark full of people who hate your guts means you've truly made it as a player. Every face in the park looks unhappy to see me.

Except one.

Josh Spencer, standing in the on-deck circle, warming up for the first at-bat. Even from a hundred feet away, the amused tilt of his lips is obvious.

We texted a lot over the last two weeks. Flirty texts. Friend texts. FaceTime calls. Jamie kept asking me why I was smiling at my phone, and I finally broke down and told him why. He laughed at me, not meanly, and said he understood the need to be discreet till we're ready to tell the world.

Now I'm smiling for another reason. Because I pulled this off. The team didn't want to put me on the roster for this game. But I begged the manager for a third time, then a fourth. "You really want to go all the way to Tampa?" My answer was simple and, evidently, enough for him, when I said, "Desperately."

Now I'm desperate for the game to be over, even though it's just begun.

Josh sets up in the batter's box, then works a walk off our pitcher. A single by another Union hitter sends him from first to third. Where I'm standing.

"Fancy running into you here," I say.

He gives me an amused look, brown eyes twinkling. "I think it's usually you plowing into me."

"Well, you can do that later."

Josh laughs, nudges me with his shoulder, and suddenly we're the only people in the ballpark, all ten thousand naysayers whisked somewhere else. Reality snaps back into focus when the Union batter swings, sending a ball down the foul line.

"Make sure you stretch first," I add. "How is the hammie?"

"Better. The docs said I was cleared for all on-field activities."

"How about off the field ones?"

"I'm supposed to go slow. Take my time. Really work all the kinks out."

"Well, if you need some help with that, be sure to let me know."

"Oh, don't worry, I will."

The batter makes contact on the next pitch, sending a line drive into the shallow outfield and Josh toward home plate with a "later" trailed as a promise.

After that, there's nothing to do but play baseball. Spring training games can go either very slowly or very fast. Slow, because no one's trying to get hurt. Fast, because if you're an everyday player, you can leave in about the fifth inning, when your work is done for the day.

I go into the dugout for the inning break, expecting to get the swat on the ass that's baseball for *good game, have a great night*. But instead the manager doesn't announce a substitution.

"I was wondering if I was staying in for the next inning," I ask him, trying not to give away my rampant desire to get the hell out of here.

He arches a brow, suspicious. "Thought you were 'desperate' to play in Tampa, Garnett."

Busted. "Just wanted to make sure you weren't pulling me. Looking forward to it."

When the announcer calls my name as the first hitter, there's another rain of boos.

My manager gestures toward the stands. "You getting what you came for?"

Not even close. "Yep, sure am," I say, then grab my bat and go to piss off a few more fans.

12

JOSH

After the game, I find Chris in the parking lot, leaning against my car. He's holding a paper bag with the neck of a champagne bottle sticking out of it.

My teammates stream out to their cars. A few call greetings to Chris. Some grumble more or less good-naturedly. Zach, our catcher, gives us a wave and a slight smile, before going to his own truck where the Gothams' catcher stands, waiting.

I thump Chris on the back in greeting. He smells clean and freshly showered, and I want to kiss him against my car the way we didn't all those months ago.

But I also want to be alone with him more.

"C'mon," he says, and opens the passenger side door.

Objectively, it's a five-minute drive from the ballpark to my condo. Subjectively, it lasts approximately five hundred years.

Chris mostly keeps his hands to himself while I'm driving. That's disappointing but probably necessary since the roads are full of Florida drivers. And also, if he touches me, I might combust.

We park at my rental apartment. I go for the door handle, but stop when Chris grabs my arm, then leans halfway across the center console.

"Hey," he says, soft. "I missed you."

"You came to Tampa to see me."

He smiles. "I did."

"And brought me champagne."

"I brought *me* champagne. Maybe I'll let you drink some though. Off me."

"Chris—"

"Yes?"

I don't say anything else, mostly because I reach for Chris just as he reaches for me. It's like touching a flame to a fuse. His lips open against mine, and his tongue finds its way into my mouth, and his shoulders are solid where he's half-draped over the console. My hand curls around the back of his neck, fingers teasing into his hair. His breath is minty, like he brushed his teeth for me, like he was getting ready for me. It's a heady thought—that the guy you want is just as eager for you too. As that idea echoes in my mind, I deepen the kiss, wanting more of his taste, more of those lips.

Just more.

As I tug on his lower lip, his breath hitches, and I groan. And then I clutch him harder, gripping him. I've got to have Chris, and I kiss him the way I feel—a little out of my mind for him.

Maybe I can't get enough of him. Maybe he likes that.

Chris pulls back, chest heaving. "Inside?"

And I nod in frantic agreement.

A few minutes later, we're in my apartment, stripped down to nothing, clothes pooled on the floor somewhere. Chris pulls me onto the bed, on top of him, and at last, at long fucking last, there's nothing between us. Just warm skin and need.

He wraps his legs around me, and grabs my face in his hands, holds me hard and rough. "Stay there."

As if I'd go anywhere.

He gets up, padding toward the bedroom

door, and I lean up on my elbows to admire the flex of muscles in his back.

Chris bends, hunting for something, then comes back holding the bottle of champagne.

I wave at it. "What's that for?"

"We never got that champagne toast."

"You think I'm gonna raise a glass to your beating us?"

"Who said anything about a glass?"

Chris works the wire cap off the bottle, then grips the cork, yanking it out. Champagne gushes onto his hand in a river of bubbles. He climbs back on the bed, kneeling over me, bottle aloft. "I know I came to Tampa to see you. I know I just spent three hours getting booed by a bunch of Florida retirees. So yeah, I'm gonna get my champagne toast."

He tips the bottle, sending champagne splashing down on my chest, then sets the bottle on the nightstand. The liquid settles in the center of my chest before running off in drips.

In a flash, he leans over me, chasing them with his mouth. When he arrives on a nipple, licking, I thread my fingers through his hair like I did on the couch in the photo studio. Delicious, mind-bending heat flares down my spine. But something about this feels not quite right. He took a team bus across the state to see me, and I want to say thank you and show my appreciation. I want to make up for the celebration we missed in October.

I sit up, sending more champagne onto the bedspread. Yes, I will be doing laundry tonight, and I'm so good with that.

"You good?" Chris asks.

I reach for the bottle, putting it in his hands. "If we're celebrating, it seems like you should get something to celebrate. Sit back. Against the headboard."

He follows my orders, and I settle between his muscular thighs, then roam my eyes over his frame. Muscles for days. Gorgeous, tan skin. A smattering of chest hair. And all those carved abs, bisected by my favorite thing. An enticing line of hair, a trail leading to his cock.

Chris reaches down, wraps his hand around the base, offering his shaft to me, wet, leaking at the tip.

I nudge the bottle where he's holding it, encouraging him to drink.

When he realizes what I'm offering, he makes a noise deep in his throat. "You gonna suck me while I'm drinking champagne?"

"When I win the World Series, you can return the favor," I tease. But I can't resist him any longer. I dip my face, swirl my tongue around the head, my eyes falling shut at that first heady, musky taste of him. He's so tempting. I rub my beard along his thighs, rub my nose over his sac, and spend a good long time licking his cock, his balls.

For a while, the only sounds are my mouth on him and the occasional swig of champagne. And his encouragement, which grows from sentences to words to a strangled gasp as I take him in my throat.

I pull back, and he grabs himself in desperation.

"I'm not above begging," Chris says, like a warning, as he thrusts the bottle onto the nightstand, grabbing the lube instead. "Seriously, just fuck me, Josh."

Like I could deny Chris now.

"Since you asked nicely," I tease. But I also really want to fuck my man.

He lies down and plants his feet wide on the bedspread, and tosses me the lube. "Want to feel you deep inside me," he says. Making all his needs clear.

My dick twitches, hard and heavy between my legs. But my focus is on him, as I drizzle the lube in my hand, then get him ready. Chris has always been so easy in his body, so in tuned to who he is. To watch him losing his mind as I open him up, his ass bumping down on my fingers, is such a privilege.

When he's sweating and panting, I set down the lube, grab a condom, and roll it on.

Chris pushes up on his elbows once more. Lifts his chin. "Kiss me," he orders and that's it.

That's all.

I kiss him deeply, then I set my hands on his thighs, push his knees up and I take my time, slowly, slowly, pushing inside. With each inch, I lower my chest closer and he seeks me out, his hands raking through my hair, brushing it off my forehead. His eyes never leaving mine.

We connect. With bodies and champagne-soaked skin. With heartbeats and unspoken promises as we come together. But words are important, especially for two guys who haven't always used the right words at the right time.

"You good?" I ask.

"So good," he murmurs.

"I want you, Chris. Again and again."

He shifts against me in answer, eyes a wide, vulnerable blue. "You have me."

Sometimes you do need words. True

ones. Words that start turning this flirtation into the real thing.

As I sink all the way inside him, this feeling of utter rightness spreads through my body, fills my bones. Chris, with his face to the side of the pillow, lets me know what he wants. I bury my face in his neck, lavishing kisses all along his warm skin, his hard dick rubbing against my stomach. He stretches his neck, telling me without words to keep kissing.

We don't fuck like the world is on fire. We fuck like we've got all the time we could ever want and like we don't want any of this to end. I go deeper in him with each thrust and he pulls me closer, our champagne-slicked chests rubbing together, my mouth on his skin. Until he says, "Wait."

I push up on my arms, bracing myself on my hands. "Everything okay?"

"I've got this fantasy," he says, rough and gravelly.

"Oh you do?"

Chris tells me how he wants me, and I close my eyes as the intensity of that image flickers before me.

"Yes. Now. Fucking now," I grunt.

We take a few seconds to maneuver around the bed so I'm on my back. He climbs over me, straddles me and lowers himself onto my shaft.

"Hold on to the headboard," he says.

I reach back, wrapping my fingers around the slats, and I let him do all the work. Like that, he works me over with his ass, driving me out of my mind with pleasure. I can't move and I don't want to, my arms straining as I hold on to the bed.

He leans down, scraping his stubble against my neck. Pressing a hot kiss to my collarbone like he did in the parking lot all those months ago.

"How's that feel?" he asks.

"So fucking good." I feel shaken up like a champagne bottle, ready to pop. But I want him to come with me. I cast my gaze down to his thick cock, leaking.

"Jack yourself," I tell him. He barely needs permission. Seconds later, his fist flies along his shaft. There is nothing hotter than Chris riding me and fucking his fist.

My balls tighten. My own climax builds, closer, closer.

When he shoots all over me, I'm just done. I come with a loud groan, the world blinking off.

Later, after we clean up, washing off champagne and sex from our bodies, then starting the laundry, we return to bed, and change the sheets. Once we flop down, I ask him a question. One that feels like it has an obvious answer, but asking matters. Asking is important. "Spend the night?"

Chris scoffs. "Dude, did you really think I was leaving?"

I shrug, maybe to hide my smile. "Just making sure."

"I begged the manager to let me play in Tampa. Fucking Tampa. And trust me, it wasn't to see the sights of the town."

I can't hide a smile now. I kiss his nose. "Good."

"Also, I noticed your hamstring was perfect. Were you ever injured at all or was that just a trick to get me here?"

I gaze down at his naked body in my bed. "Seems it worked. Told you I wasn't stupid."

"I don't know. You might need to prove it to me," Chris says.

I roll over, pinning him. Pressing kisses to his neck, his shoulder, his jaw. "I'll prove it when you come over after our opening day game. Maybe the next night too."

"Josh Spencer, are you trying to lock me down?"

No point even trying to play it cool. Stoic me has left the building. "Yes. Yes, I am."

Chris just shrugs, laidback and easy, but his smile gives him away. It's a whole new one —magnetic as always, but intimate. Just for me. "Good," he says. "Let's keep it that way."

I plan to.

EPILOGUE
CHRIS

Opening Day

Four weeks later, Josh comes to the plate in the Gothams ballpark. He's carrying his bat and, from the way he strides into the batter's box, the weight of the world. Or maybe he's just bringing along the memory of the last time our teams played against each other.

The fifty thousand screaming Gothams fans probably don't help. Even from where I'm standing on third base, I can see the determined set of his mouth. Our pitcher winds up and throws an arcing curveball that Josh swings at and misses.

If I thought this place was loud before, now it's thunderous. I almost feel bad. But not bad enough. I hope he strikes out—or better yet, hits one right at me so I can throw him out.

I don't get my wish, because he connects on the next pitch, sending the ball swooping into an outfield corner. Our right fielder scrambles after it, and Josh breaks for first, rounding it, then doesn't slow as he passes second and heads toward me. Hustling out a triple.

My teammate hurls the ball across the diamond toward me. And Josh does what any good base runner would during that play. He slides.

Into me.

His cleats spike my ankle. I jump back, but not before attempting—and failing—to get a tag on him.

The umpire calls him safe.

Josh lies in the dirt, out of breath from running hard. I could let him stay there.

Instead I offer him a hand up.

The leather of his batting glove is smooth against my palm as he levers himself up.

"Nice night for some baseball, huh, Garnett," he says.

We haven't seen each other, except on FaceTime, since that night in Tampa. Four more weeks in Florida that apparently agreed with him, because he looks tan, thick with muscle, his beard cropped close. And I want to say a bunch of things to him, like *your place or mine* but there's the small issue of an umpire behind us plus fifty thousand fans.

"You doing anything after the game?" I ask.

Josh pretends to consider it. "Someone once called me a baseball monk. So you know, early night at the monastery."

"Nothing I could to do persuade you to go out? I'm told I can be convincing."

"More like persistent."

"Some of us can go hard for hours."

And I swear the third base umpire makes a slightly strangled sound.

"Well, I know one thing I probably have to do tonight," Josh says. "Answer questions about our supposed feud to the New York media."

I scan the stands on the third base line. "You think anyone noticed you slid into me?"

"Nah, probably not," he jokes. "Both our fanbases are known for their completely level-headed reactions to sports. Doubt anyone will even say anything."

After the game, I stand in front of my stall in the clubhouse for the usual post-game scrum. Of course, all anyone asks me is about the slide. "Spencer got me pretty good in the ankle," I say. "It happens. Decided not to make a federal case about it."

Gently razzing the Union player only encourages the media. "Any response to what Spencer said about the slide a few minutes ago?" a reporter asks.

I decide to wind up the press even further. "Wouldn't know what he said. It's not like we spend all our time sending videos to each other." Which is technically true. We spend *some* time doing that. But I also have to sleep and play baseball.

One of the reporters for The Sports Network hands me her phone. On it, a video plays of Josh. He's standing in front of a similar crowd of reporters, probably a few minutes ago. I throw the group around me a smile. "There's no chance I can watch this without an audience?"

I watch the clip as a reporter off-camera asks Josh why he slid into third tonight.

"Just trying to hustle out a triple," he says, scrubbing a hand over that beard I'm going to feel against my face in a few more minutes. "I got pretty winded rounding second, so it made sense to come in feet first."

"But you weren't happy when Garnett did

something similar last October," the reporter prompts.

"I wasn't," Josh says, looking contrite. "Losing the World Series sucks. But I shouldn't have made it about Garnett either. Sometimes, you just get beat, fair and square. That's what happened in October. And I told Garnett as much in the off-season. But that was on me for letting it go on as long as it did . . ." He takes a beat, looks straight at the camera, maybe even at me in a way, then adds, "I guess . . . he's a nice guy."

The video ends, and I'm met with interrogating media eyes.

"So no more bad blood between you?" a thirtysomething print reporter asks.

I smile. That's one way to put it. "Yeah, everything's good between Spencer and me. We made sure to kiss and make up."

And with that, I bid the reporters good night.

EPILOGUE
JOSH

One month is a long time.

So I arranged for a town car.

With a partition.

The second the sleek black vehicle pulls away from the ballpark, I pounce on Chris. I'm pent up, coiled with need, and I unleash it.

I claim Chris's mouth, kissing him deep and hot. Our teeth click, and I can barely keep track of where his hands are, where mine are.

Except . . . all over each other. I tug at his shirt, yank at the waistband. My hands slide up his strong chest, and I break the kiss to drag my nose along his neck. He smells so good, tastes even better. My brain goes hazy, already intoxicated by that clean, post-game, showered smell, and by my own ravenous need to reconnect.

I break the kiss to murmur across his lips. "Four goddamn weeks," I say, then drag his lower lip between my teeth, sucking, then skating my tongue into his mouth.

Chris lets out a feral groan, chased with a laugh.

A delicious laugh that I missed. Along with everything else about him. As he coasts his lips over mine, he whispers back at me, "Missed you so fucking much."

With my head in a fog, I half wonder how this has happened. How we went from that golf tournament nearly a year ago, to all those games, to the series, to the photoshoot, to spring training, to now.

Making out with abandon, after midnight, in the backseat of a car.

Then I stop wondering because the answer is in my arms.

The answer is instinct, connection, trust.

Eventually, I figured out how to trust my own instincts with Chris Garnett.

They tell me that I want him tonight, tomorrow, and for a long, long time. That settles my rocketing pulse, knowing this is the start of us coming together, again and again.

I downshift, running my thumb over his late-night stubble, kissing him slowly. He chases my lips. A brand-new sensation pulses through my body—a buzzy, giddy feeling borne from the desire to have him *and* to keep him.

Maybe we both feel it at the same time since we settle into a new rhythm, luxuriating in each other's kisses along the I-87.

When we near my neighborhood, he breaks the kiss. "I like what you said tonight," he tells me.

"Good. I wanted you to see it," I say.

"I told them we kissed and made up," Chris says, with a sly grin.

"Truer words," I say. "Maybe when we do the golf tournament in a few weeks, you'll kiss me on the course."

"You're right. I probably will."

I glance toward the tinted window. "You were right about the traffic too."

"I'm right about a lot of things, Josh."

Chris loops a hand around my head, curls his fingers through my hair, then draws me close one more time. I'm expecting another epic make-out session over the last few blocks. Instead, he says, "Like how good we are together."

I count down the seconds until we're inside my apartment, the door shutting, the world closing off.

Until it's just us, my rival and me, on top of the city, all the what-ifs fading away into the New York sky, swept away into the dark, as I bring him home.

THE END

Want to be the first to learn of sales, new releases, preorders and special freebies from Lauren Blakely and KD Casey? Sign up for our exclusive MM VIP mailing list here! We have some amazing deals you won't want to miss. Plus, be sure to preorder Dirty Steal, the next scorching hot standalone in our Dirty Players series!

A sexy, one-bed-in-the-room/friends-to-lovers standalone romance!
I expected a lot of things out of this season: to bat third for my team. To compete for a World Series ring. To fight like hell to win.
Check. Check. Check.

What I didn't expect? My childhood best friend to show up in my dugout, courtesy of a trade to my team. Or for him to need a place to stay. I offer him mine, since we're just friends.

It'll be good, clean fun.

Right?

Except I didn't plan on him stealing my spot in the line up. And I definitely didn't plan on him stealing my heart.

Preorder Dirty Steal!

Intrigued by Chris's friend Jamie DeLuca? What's his story with Big Mack? Find out all the delicious details in KD Casey's sultry, sexy, veteran/rookie romance One True Outcome, available everywhere! And if you were intrigued by Grant Blackwood, his romance is told in Lauren Blakely's Men of Summer series, a sexy, emotional, epic romance you won't want to miss!

Zach Glasser's story is told in KD Casey's Unwritten Rules. Read on for an exclusive sneak peek at KD's novel One True Outcome for more of Jamie's sexy romance...

Here's a sneak peek of **One True Outcome**!

Mack flies to Florida on a tiny pill of a charter plane. Their flight path takes him on a wide swoop over the blue expanse of the Florida ocean before depositing him on the tarmac at Miami-Dade International. It's hot, hotter even than the worst days in Baltimore, a kind of humid airlessness that makes Mack understand snowbirds who only come to the city when it's not baseball season.

A handler from the team greets him, ushering him into a town car that lurches through Miami traffic. She apologizes for the road congestion like it's her fault, and he wonders about the kinds of assholes she's responsible for ushering around if that's her reaction. Or the kind of asshole she expects him to be.

"I thought I was gonna have to take an Uber," he says, "and I always end up in a two-door. So this is better."

She gives him an amused look like she's trying to imagine him fitting into a normal-sized car—which is admittedly difficult with his height and bulk—and then offers him champagne hidden in one of the side compartments.

At the stadium, he's ushered through a series of meetings: with Myra, the team president, who lays out the contract terms they'll offer. With the coaching staff, who discuss his potential role as a tandem first basemen and occasional pinch hitter. And of course, they welcome his expertise at the plate and whatever wisdom he's willing to impart to young hitters.

Don't end up like me, kids, Mack doesn't say, and just nods and says he understands.

They parade him into the clubhouse, into the changing area that's lined with expensive wooden stalls, each with its own padded leather rolling chair parked in front of it.

"We hope you don't mind," Myra says, because there's a stall with Mack's name on a placard above it, a set of Swordfish gear that will either be his or the world's least valuable collectables. "I'll leave you to get acquainted with some of our players."

There's a guy hovering near his stall, shifting his weight between his feet like he doesn't want Mack to know he's hovering.

Mack doesn't recognize him, but he's built like a catcher, stocky, especially in his lower half. Short, at least for a ballplayer, and certainly shorter than Mack at 6'5", and at least a decade younger than he is. He has sandy brown hair that glints under the clubhouse lighting, olive skin that shows a slight flush, and an open expression, like the game hasn't yet worn him down. They haven't even said anything to one another yet, and Mack gets the urge to tell him to hold onto that while he can.

He's also looking at Mack with the wide-eyed recognition that fans get at events, ones where Mack has to do most of the talking or, alternatively, just politely nods when they tell him about that time they saw him way back when. Encounters that end with an encouragement to buck up, like all he needs is a change in attitude.

"Hi," Mack says, because otherwise he and whoever this is will just be in a staring contest. He nods to the stall the team created for him, which feels slightly like a diorama he made in grade school, something made to be disassembled. "This is a pretty nice set up. Which one's yours?"

The kid glances over his shoulder, like Mack was addressing someone behind him. He points to a nearby stall, one with jerseys reading "DeLuca" hung up neatly.

"Nice to meet you, DeLuca," Mack says.

"Um, James is fine. Or DeLuca. Or Jamie. Or 'Luke.'"

"Which is it?"

DeLuca cuts a smile at him, the kind of smile that would look a little sarcastic if not accompanied by a slight flush to his cheeks. "'Jamie' is fine. If you want."

Another player comes over, Gonzalez, who Mack recognizes from when they played together in the World Baseball Classic. Gonzalez throws an arm around Jamie's shoulders and gives him an honest-to-god noogie, which Jamie squirms at.

"What DeLuca is trying to say is that he had your poster on his wall growing up," Gonzalez says. "And he's trying to ask for your autograph."

Jamie's cheeks go an even brighter red. "Gonzo, stop it."

Gonzalez to his credit, does stop. Other players, sensing both an opportunity to razz a teammate and avoid anything resembling work, start drifting over.

And Mack was in a clubhouse all of five days ago, but he's overwhelmed by the nostalgia at being back in one. Guys clap him on the arm and ask him if he's gonna sign with Miami—and don't get that flicker of worry when he says he's considering it. Like it wouldn't be the worst thing to have him play there.

He gets lost in the swirl of conversation, players cycling in and out before they grudgingly go to lifting sessions or to get worked on by trainers. Jamie doesn't move from where he's standing next to him. He's older than Mack first guessed, probably in his mid-twenties or so, but with the air of everyone's kid brother. Other players rib him, poking him in the sides or dragging their fingers through his hair, and if he's a catcher, Mack has no idea how he's managing the pitching staff.

He also occasionally casts a look at Mack like he really does want that autograph. Or more probably, wants Mack to be the player he was supposed to be, the perpetual super-star whose career instead dimmed.

A reminder that, even if Miami invited him down to plead their case, he doesn't have many other options. Or really any other options. If things don't work out here, he'll probably end up at his mother's house on the Gulf Coast to live out his days among the other retirees.

Eventually the novelty of his visit wears off, and guys start saying their goodbyes. Mack issues a few hugs to players he knows, a few awkward waves to ones he doesn't, and then it's him and Jamie left there.

"I'm, uh, supposed to give you a tour," Jamie says.

"You draw the short straw?"

"Not exactly." Another flush, this one accompanied by a slightly bitten lip, and a promise to show Mack the wonders of Miami's ballpark.

They tour the clubhouse, Jamie showing him its various features, though Mack's been in enough clubhouses over the years that he could probably navigate this one in the dark. They go down the hallway to the weight room, which Jamie introduces with a little flick of gesture, a ta-da like a magician at a child's birthday party.

"These are, um, the weights," he says. And then immediately seems to realize what he's done, scrubbing his palm over his face.

It's charming, in part because most other players, have been so distinctly unimpressed by Mack for so long. The kind of adoration Mack found overwhelming when he was young, then irritating, then finally just evaporated like midday sweat.

Jamie looks like he's torn between wanting to finish the tour and wanting the tiled floor to open and swallow him whole. Mack decides to take pity on him.

"How long did you say you'd been with the Swordfish?" Mack asks, though Jamie hadn't said one way or another.

He gives Mack a flash of what might be gratitude for the subject change. "This'll be my first full year in the bigs." He looks like he might append the answer with a *sir*. Which Mack is grateful he doesn't and he tells himself that it's because it'd make him feel older than dirt and not for any other reason. Especially when Jamie wets his lips, which are full and slightly chapped in the over-air-conditioned clubhouse, after he says it.

"I was in the minors for a few years," Jamie adds.

"Catcher development takes time. I don't

know if folks remember, but I got drafted as a catcher."

"I know," Jamie says, quickly. "Gonzo wasn't, um, actually joking. About the poster thing. Sorry, I know that's probably weird. This is hard 'cause I'm used to you being..." He trails off.

"On TV?"

"Something like that." Jamie's shoulders ease from where they're up by his ears. "C'mon, I'll show you the field. It has grass and bases and everything."

Mack laughs at that. "I'm sure I'll love it."

Preorder the novel One True Outcome!

A veteran player on a new team. The rookie who hero-worshiped him growing up. The unwritten rule they're about to break.

Everyone knows you don't fall for a teammate. Especially the rookie you're supposed to mentor. Tell that to Matt "Big Mack" Mackenzie though. Now at the tail end of his career, the one-time superstar takes an offer from the only team willing to give him a shot.

The hook? The job includes extra practice sessions with the team's rookie catcher. The tempting, smart-mouthed Jamie DeLuca, who Mack really shouldn't think about that way. And he definitely shouldn't agree to after-hours video review sessions with.

The sky's the limit for Jamie, if only he can keep his spot in the lineup. But the rookie's on the verge of being cut. If he wants to stay on a big league roster that'll mean extra work —and extra time with Big Mack. The guy he fantasized about playing like growing up. And then just fantasized about.

Mack's nothing like Jamie's fantasies. He's *better*. If only Jamie could keep his attraction to the charming, generous veteran under wraps. Easier said than done, especially when the heat between them ignites.

· · ·

But nothing in baseball comes with a guarantee—and the only outcome they can be certain of is the one they make for themselves.

ALSO BY LAUREN BLAKELY

FULL PACKAGE, the #1 New York Times
Bestselling romantic comedy!

BIG ROCK, the hit New York Times Bestselling
standalone romantic comedy!

THE SEXY ONE, a New York Times Bestselling
standalone romance!

THE KNOCKED UP PLAN, a multi-week USA
Today and Amazon Charts Bestselling standalone
romance!

MOST VALUABLE PLAYBOY, a sexy multi-week
USA Today Bestselling sports romance! And its
companion sports romance, MOST LIKELY TO
SCORE!

WANDERLUST, a USA Today Bestselling
contemporary romance!

COME AS YOU ARE, a Wall Street Journal and
multi-week USA Today Bestselling contemporary
romance!

PART-TIME LOVER, a multi-week USA Today
Bestselling contemporary romance!

UNBREAK MY HEART, an emotional second chance USA Today Bestselling contemporary romance!

BEST LAID PLANS, a sexy friends-to-lovers USA Today Bestselling romance!

The Heartbreakers! The USA Today and WSJ Bestselling rock star series of standalone!

P.S. IT'S ALWAYS BEEN YOU, a sweeping, second chance romance!

MY ONE WEEK HUSBAND, a sexy standalone romance!

ALSO BY KD CASEY

ONE TRUE OUTCOME, a sexy, veteran/rookie romance!

UNWRITTEN RULES, an emotional second-chance baseball romance debut!

CONTACT

You can find Lauren on Twitter at Lauren-Blakely3, Instagram at LaurenBlakelyBooks, Facebook at LaurenBlakelyBooks, or online at LaurenBlakely.com. You can also email her at laurenblakelybooks@gmail.com

KD Casey would love to hear from you! Find her on Twitter, Instagram, and Facebook at KDCaseyWrites, online at kdcaseywrites.com, or email at kdcaseywrites@gmail.com.

Printed in Great Britain
by Amazon

40364221R00086